AN ACCIDENTAL CHRISTMAS

ITALIAN ROMANCE
BOOK FOUR

DIANA FRASER

An Accidental Christmas
by Diana Fraser

© 2017 Diana Fraser
dianafraser.com

—Italian Romance—
The Italian's Perfect Lover
Seduced by the Italian
The Passionate Italian
An Accidental Christmas

Authors note: The traditions and setting for *An Accidental Christmas* were inspired by the real town of Abbadia san Salvatore, but the town and people in this book, are purely a product of my own invention.

DEDICATION

To Mum and Dad, with much love always.

CHAPTER 1

Ursula watched the sleek Ferrari, its front grill festooned with flowers and ribbons, drive away from the Montecorvio Rovella estate. There was a backward glance from both Alessandro and Emily, a wave, and then they were gone.

She sighed. Emily's eyes had held hers momentarily before Alessandro had commanded her attention. They'd radiated happiness that only briefly dimmed when they'd caught Ursula's gaze. Sympathy. She hated it.

"Now *they* are a couple in love."

The woman speaking was hushed by her friend and turned round puzzled until she caught sight of Ursula. Ursula recognized her as Simone, an old friend of Alessandro's whom she knew only slightly. Simone fell into step beside Ursula, as they walked over to the cars.

"So, are you returning to Sweden for Christmas?" Simone asked.

Ursula had been, but suddenly she couldn't face it. Her father, stepmother and her teenage half-sisters wouldn't miss her. They didn't need her to complete their family at Christmas. Her married friends had extended kind invitations for Ursula to join them, but they all had their own families. They'd all be looking at her wondering why the girl they'd known at boarding school as "the girl likeliest to succeed," was alone at Christmas.

She smiled—the smile that could always be counted on to disguise her real thoughts and emotions. "No. I thought I might stay in Italy."

"Christmas with friends. Sounds good. Christmas with family is so often fraught with issues."

Ursula nodded, unwilling to tell her that Christmas without family *or* friends was what she was seeking. "It makes a change."

"Whereabouts are you going?"

Ursula thought quickly. "North." She hoped the vague destination would suffice. She'd hoped wrong.

"The coast?"

"No." Just the idea of retracing the holidays she'd had with Alessandro along Italy's coast tightened the knot in her gut. "No," she repeated more firmly. "The mountains."

"Ah, good idea. You should stop off in Abbadia San Alexis on your way. It has amazing medieval buildings. And the frescoes—Emily would love them." Simone stopped speaking abruptly, suddenly realizing what she'd said.

Ursula smiled. "It's okay, you know. Emily and I are good friends. Alessandro and I broke up long before Emily came along."

Simone's relief was palpable. "Oh, yeah, I realize that. Anyhow, you should stop off in Abbadia if you've time."

Ursula smiled again as she tried to hide the vast

expanse of emptiness that had been resting deep inside, buried until now. It had taken the wedding of two of her closest friends to uncover it. "Sure. Well, I'd best be off."

She said her goodbyes, and walked over to her rental car.

No-one was looking at her now, and she could allow the void which had been revealed at seeing Alessandro so in love with someone else, to find its place in the dead center of her heart. She didn't have to pretend anymore. She was happy for Alessandro. She *was*. They weren't just words to reassure everyone. But it had been *Alessandro* who'd called off their relationship; it had been *Alessandro* who hadn't loved her enough, and it had been *her* who'd been left wondering why.

She couldn't help it. She hadn't been enough for him, she hadn't been enough for her previous boyfriend who'd finished their relationship with a text and she doubted she'd be enough for anyone. Despite what all the school yearbooks stated, despite all the advances from people who shouldn't be flirting with her, despite how busy she kept herself, there was an emptiness in the place where her heart should have been.

It had died a little with each rejection. Beginning with when she'd been sent to live with her grandparents as a child after her parent's divorce, continuing with when she'd been packed off to an elite boarding school at eleven years of age, and sealed with the rejections of men who'd been unable, or unwilling, to see beyond the exterior she'd created to hide behind.

She needed to leave her world, just for a while. She needed to come to terms with the fact that she didn't believe that emptiness would ever be filled.

She'd head north, as she'd told Simone. She suddenly remembered her friend Ruby would be in Florence for New Year. She'd find someplace to hide out for Christmas and then she'd go to Florence. Now, where was the place Simone had mentioned? She couldn't remember, but it didn't matter. She'd just drive.

THE TRAFFIC WAS BARELY MOVING along the coastal highway. The rain, which had begun as soon as Ursula had left Naples, had turned to sleet, and red tail lights pierced the gloom as far as she could see. She checked her dashboard; the temperature had plummeted. Some holiday. At least she'd managed to contact Ruby and arrange to meet in early January. It was only just over a week away. She'd find something between now and then if she ever got out of this traffic jam, that was.

She peered at the unfamiliar gear stick, and crunched the car into gear as the line of traffic edged forward. She looked up just as the brake lights of the vehicle in front flared. She slammed on the brakes and sat, motor running, listening to yet another irritating Christmas song on the radio. Of course. What did she expect when she tried to drive through the rush hour at the beginning of the Christmas holiday season? The one time she decides to do something impromptu, and it backfires.

The traffic crawled briefly before stopping again. Ursula banged her fists impotently on the steering wheel. She couldn't do this. It was making her crazy. All she wanted to do was put her foot hard on the accelerator and drive away from everything that was haunting her.

She gripped the wheel. She had to get off the main road. Anywhere. As a small road approached on the right, she signaled and turned into it. She didn't even know where it was going. It was enough for her that it was leading away from Rome. She just wanted to drive, to follow her nose and stop only at nightfall where she could be away from everyone. Only her, in some anonymous, nameless hotel. There, she'd wait for Christmas to be over.

Lost in her thoughts as she negotiated the winding mountain road, away from all the traffic now, Ursula was hardly aware of the change in the light. The sleet had turned into airy snowflakes which drifted slowly down from an iron-gray sky. It wasn't until she continued onwards, up through thickening trees—their branches already weighed down by snow—that the snow began to accumulate on the windscreen and Ursula realized this was more than just a passing snow shower. She peered out at the white world around her and smiled to herself as she absorbed its sheer beauty.

At a bend in the road, she pulled over into a siding, thick with newly fallen snow. She switched the engine off, and stepped out into a world of white. There was no sound, just the soft brush of giant snowflakes as they drifted down onto her upturned face. She laughed, unable to resist sticking out her tongue and tasting them, as she'd done as a child. The whiteness of the wooded valley, with its steep sides to which the road clung, was alleviated only by dark streaks on the sheltered side of the tree trunks, downwind from the snow. They looked as if they'd been touched by the brush of an artist.

Above the steep side of the mountain, with its forest of white-cloaked chestnut trees plunging down into the valley below, the view faded out into a snow-filled sky. It was an unspoiled landscape and a strangely calming one. She was glad she'd come, even if she was lost. She shivered, pulled her coat more tightly around her and stamped her feet which were beginning to numb with cold. Time to go. Climbing back into the car, she turned on the ignition but, instead of an engine roaring into life, there was only an ominous whirring sound that sent a sickening chill into her stomach.

She got out, opened up the bonnet and gave it a cursory look. Why, she didn't know because she had no idea what she was looking for. She let it fall with a clang and looked around. The snow was settling deeper now, and no recent tracks disturbed its pristine beauty. For the first time, she felt a stab of concern. She tried her cell phone again. There was no reception. If only she'd paid more attention to the road signs giving a destination, or a historic site, *anything* that could have given her some sense of where she was in this landscape devoid of people or houses. But she hadn't. She looked uphill to where the road disappeared around a corner, into a wall of white. It had to lead somewhere. She decided she'd walk for half an hour and, if there were no signs of life, she'd return to the car.

She grabbed her bags, locked the car and began walking, trundling the case behind her on the snowy road. Half an hour passed, and her light coat was wet through. Her boots were starting to chafe her feet, and not one car had gone by. The snow began to fall more heavily. She dragged the case behind her on the snowy road. Her Gucci handbag was soaked, she thought glumly. The suede would never recover.

Then she heard something. A rumbling. She stopped and turned around, but couldn't see anything through the thickly falling snow. She shivered, whether through fear or cold she couldn't have said. She rarely felt vulnerable, but she did now.

A puff of exhaust rose from around the bend, and a tractor emerged, its headlamps blinding in the snow, pulling behind it a trailer load of wood. It wasn't until it drew up beside her that she saw the outline of a solitary man in the driver's seat, seemingly oblivious to the cold and wet. She couldn't see anything of him beneath the broad hat, and the turned-up collar of his thick coat.

"*Caio!*" he called.

"*Caio!*" she responded.

"Is that your car, a couple of miles back there?"

"Yes, it won't start."

"Climb up. I'll take you to where you'll get cellphone coverage. I can't turn around on this road, but I'll come back later and tow the car to town."

"Thank you so much! I was beginning to think I'd have to spend the night in the car."

"You might have had to if I hadn't been late collecting wood." He extended his hand, she gripped it and he pulled her up beside him. Face to face, she could see his eyes were as warm as the hand which enveloped hers. There wasn't much room and, when she sat down, his leg pressed against hers. "You're cold. You'd better get under this." He dragged a blanket—an old dog blanket that had seen better days by the smell of things—from behind them. She covered herself gingerly, still shivering despite its scratchy protection. "My name is Demetrio Pecora."

"Ursula. Ursula Adamsson."

He released the brake, revved the accelerator and the tractor scrunched safely over the thick snow. As they rounded a bend in the road the wind increased, sending the snow shooting horizontally across their path. Ursula shivered, and pulled the blanket higher over her head, clasping it tightly around her neck. She glanced at Demetrio, whose only response to the sudden snow storm, was a narrowing of his eyes. With his eyes hidden, and a hat pulled low over his brow, all that was visible was the side of his face—tanned, a shadow of stubble and a strong jawline.

She looked away quickly, feeling uncomfortable with this enforced intimacy with a stranger who, she now realized, had the sort of looks more usually seen on the pages of a magazine. She looked around, trying to think of a topic of conversation. "That's a lot of firewood you have in the back."

He glanced at her, his lips curving into a smile. Her heart quickened, and she looked away, worried for the first time in a long time that she might blush. "*Si*. We're big on bonfires here at Christmas."

"And where is 'here?'" She kept her eyes firmly on the snowy landscape.

"Abbadia San Alexis."

The place she'd been advised to go earlier! Of course, it was.

She groaned. It seemed fate had decided where she was going, whether she liked it or not.

"Didn't you know where you were?"

She considered for a moment. "You know? I think I probably did."

They turned a corner, and he looked at her again and this time he didn't look away. "That's a strange answer."

"This is a strange holiday." She grinned. "Someone suggested I visit Abbadia San Alexis, but I hadn't thought any more about it until I turned off the highway, trying to avoid the holiday traffic. And here I am anyway."

"And here you are. With a stranger, on a tractor, under a dog's blanket."

"Yes. I couldn't have planned this if I'd tried."

"And you normally plan your life better?"

"Absolutely. My life is *always* planned. Until now, until these holidays, that is. But I think I'd better go back to planning, it's more reliable."

"Less interesting though."

"Yeah, there is that." She met his grin with one of his own, and she felt a low spreading warmth in the pit of her stomach.

"One thing planning is helpful with is accommodation. You have no accommodation booked, I assume?"

"You assume right. Do you think that'll be a problem?"

"*Si*. We can try the hotels, but Abbadia San Alexis is well known for its Christmas festival, and the town is usually full over the holiday period. But we'll sort something out."

Ursula wondered how exactly this stranger was going to sort things out for her. She should be more worried but, for some inexplicable reason, she felt reassured, happy to cast her fate into the hands of this man. At least for now.

They eventually emerged from the chestnut forest into

the medieval heart of Abbadia San Alexis—the square in front of the Abbey, which was full of people. Ursula realized why there was no one on the road—they were all here.

The square's medieval and renaissance houses of gray stone appeared untouched by time. "It's beautiful."

"The abbey dates from the eleventh century. It used to be an important station on the *Via Francigena*, a pilgrim route from northern Europe to Rome. So we're used to people passing through. Although most people know where they're coming to," he teased.

"The accidental pilgrim, that's me. Maybe God has something special lined up for me." She grinned.

His eyes lingered on her. "I wouldn't be at all surprised." The teasing note in his voice had disappeared. He pulled on the handbrake. "I have to drop off the wood. They need it for the bonfires, and then we'll try the hotels."

Ursula suddenly felt guilty. "You've done more than enough already. If you show me where to go, I can check out the hotels."

"I'm sure you can. But I'd like to help."

She began to protest. She had always been fiercely independent but, for once, she found herself nodding in agreement, persuaded by those melting brown eyes. "Okay, then. Thank you."

The medieval square was alive with people of all ages. Some were busy building the bonfires while others milled around the street stalls, shouting encouragement to the bonfire builders.

Ursula watched as Demetrio unloaded the wood, depositing it in the center of the square. From here, others took it and began erecting a square-shaped bonfire. The big logs were placed in layers of around five meters high, and the smaller firewood was slotted in between. When the last of the logs had been unloaded, they stood back and watched as the huge bonfire began to take shape.

"How high will it be?" Ursula asked.

"Up to around 30 stacks. It has to burn until dawn."

"Is it some kind of pilgrims' tradition?"

"A *villagers'* tradition. Every Christmas Eve we light fires. The Festival of *Fiaccole Della Notte di Natale* is said to have been going on for a thousand years. It's meant to have started with the villagers who lived around the Abbey. They lit fires to warm themselves as they played out the role of the shepherds who followed the star on the night of Christ's birth."

"Wow. That's very different to my hometown. The most traditional we get is buying expensive presents no one needs."

"And where is your hometown? Somewhere in Sweden?"

"I'm surprised you recognize my accent."

"I don't. But you have a Swedish name. But you're not from Sweden?"

"Oh yes, I was born there. But my accent left me years ago when I was sent to boarding school in England."

He frowned. "Boarding school? That must have been tough. How old were you?"

"Eleven." She shrugged, not wanting to turn back the clock and remember the desperate sadness she'd felt. "But that's okay. I learned to be a citizen of the world, not restricted to one place. I travel with my job and have apartments in Stockholm and New York. I have no place I call home, and that's how I like it."

Her confident tone didn't appear to convince him. "Really?"

"Yes, really. Anyway, what else happens here?"

He nodded, accepting her change of conversation. "We have a torch-lit parade which winds through the town. The torches are then used to light the stacks. We sing as we walk, obviously."

"Obviously. A parade isn't a parade without a song."

"Exactly. I can see you understand our ways already. And then, of course, we eat and drink. The local *enoteche* are all open and provide wine, and there's fantastic food in the cafés."

"It sounds wonderful."

"It *is* wonderful. Will you stay for the celebrations?"

She shrugged. "I'd love to, but I guess it depends on accommodation."

"Let's go and check it out. This way." He guided her through the busy square to a hotel across from the abbey.

It seemed entirely natural as they made their way through the crowds for him to reach for her hand and for her to accept it. Otherwise, she reasoned, they'd have become separated. And she didn't want to be lost twice in one day. And nor, it seemed, did he want to lose her.

The hotel was packed with tourists drinking at the bar. She followed Demetrio to the reception where he exchanged a few words in rapid Italian with the concierge whose shaking head and laughter made Ursula realize that she was out of luck.

"No room anywhere," Demetrio explained. "But come, have a drink to warm yourself."

"Thanks. But it's beginning to get dark. I'll need to get my car looked at."

"Ursula, there's no accommodation and certainly no garage mechanic who will leave his drink to venture into the mountains at this hour. No, come over to the fire while I get us some drinks."

"But Demetrio, I need to find somewhere to stay even if I can't get my car sorted."

"What you're overlooking is that you've found yourself a resourceful man, not only with a plan but also with parents who have a spare room."

"Your parents? But—"

"Sit by the fire." He shrugged off his wet jacket. "Here, you take this, and I'll get you a drink, and then I'll explain."

Faced with the choice of trudging through the snow to stare helplessly at a car engine in the dark, or sitting by the fire and drinking with a handsome stranger, she decided her independence shouldn't get in the way of reason. Not this time, anyway.

She peeled off her coat and hung it, together with his jacket, on the back of their chairs. Then she squeezed into the small nook seat by the roaring fire and soaked up its heat. Demetrio was right; she *was* chilled. She flexed her cold hands in front of the flames while she watched Demetrio wend his way between the jostling groups of people to the bar.

He was taller than most, and his much-washed checked shirt hung in soft folds from broad shoulders. With his hat off, she could see his hair—dark, curling and a shade too long. She sat back, lulled by the soothing heat of the fire. Hair too long for what, she thought? For a corporate boardroom, yes. But for a farmer, who'd brought her in from the cold? She sighed. For someone like that, his hair was the perfect length.

He turned and caught her eye, smiled, and raised the two large glasses of red wine above the crowds as he made his way back to her.

He sat down, by necessity, close—so close the heat from his thigh warmed hers—and raised his glass to hers. "Happy Christmas, Ursula! I hope you enjoy your stay here."

She clinked her glass against his. "I'm enjoying it already."

And she was. She could see him better now, even under the subdued lighting of the bar. With his olive skin, Roman nose and hair tumbling around his face, framing his dark eyes, he looked like he'd just stepped out of a renaissance painting. She had to force herself not to stare.

"Good, so am I. I hadn't anticipated joining in the festivities so early. Not while there's work to do."

She sipped the red wine as she enjoyed the sensation of the heat bringing life back to her chilled limbs. "I'm sorry if I'm stopping you from your work."

"It doesn't matter. It can wait until tomorrow."

"So what work should you be doing at this hour? It's dark outside already."

"There's always something to do on the farm. But it's okay. My family will have realized I've been delayed and have brought the animals in by now."

Ursula's heart sunk. Of course. He had a family waiting for him. No doubt a wife and children. She took another sip, her throat a little tighter now. She tried to smile. "Family? Your mother and father?"

"And all the rest. The farmhouse is always crowded at Christmas."

Ursula didn't say anything, hoping he'd describe precisely who his family comprised of. But it seemed Demetrio wasn't about to elaborate.

"Now," he continued, shifting in his seat, so he was half-facing her, his elbow on the back of the nook seat. "I have a proposition for you."

Ursula's stomach did a curious flip, and she focused on taking another sip of wine. "A proposition? That sounds interesting." She glanced at him and couldn't help noticing his disarming grin was back in place.

He inclined his head towards hers until their foreheads were almost touching. "I hope so."

His voice was low, and she felt it more than heard it. She struggled to take a calming breath. "This proposition, does it include a place to stay?"

"It does indeed. Would you believe my parents have a spare room over a stable?"

She laughed, relieved to break the sexual tension that was threatening to derail her senses. "That's a terrible joke."

"It would be if it were a joke. But seriously, there *is* a guest room, and it *is*, believe it or not, above the old stables." He laughed. "Don't look at me like that. Would I put you anywhere near a working stable?" He plucked off a few stray dog hairs from her angora sweater. "You, with your fine clothes and"—his gaze dropped to her suede bag now soaked through and permanently stained—"ruined designer handbag."

"Honestly? I think you might. But I'm very grateful to

you, whatever condition it's in, and I accept your kind offer. Do you think your parents will mind?"

"Mama will be thrilled to feed another person. And Papa would shoot me if he thought I hadn't helped a lady in distress."

"Your parents sound very generous."

"They are. It's a gift I've inherited." Again that grin that did strange things to her stomach. "That's settled then. Now, I'll have missed dinner at home, so would you like to join me for dinner here?"

It would have been rude to refuse.

THE SNOW HAD STOPPED FALLING by the time they stepped outside, and the temperature had dropped to below freezing. Ursula shivered in her thin coat and brought it tighter around her. Demetrio offered his arm. "You might slip in those boots," he said, by way of explanation. "You're not exactly dressed for the snow."

It was entirely logical, she thought, as she accepted his arm, and they walked through the square, quieter now the excitement of the Christmas Eve preparations was over, and everyone had returned to their homes. And, as he squeezed her arm against his body, she couldn't help feeling that it was also perfectly lovely.

The snow had settled on the cobblestones, on the rooftops, and on the overhangs and ledges of the shops; everywhere was topped and edged in startling white. Even the stars, when she looked upward, were bright in the dark sky. As she walked in step with Demetrio through the thick snow, Ursula suddenly realized she felt very happy. She couldn't remember the last time she'd felt this way.

"What's brought a smile to your face?"

"Just one of those rare moments, you know, when you look around, and everything seems just right."

"For you, these moments are rare?" He grunted but didn't press for a response. Instead, he stopped in front of a huge bonfire, edged with snow. "So… what do you think?"

"It looks amazing."

"I'll look even more amazing tomorrow night when it's lit. The kids love it."

Ursula felt her smile slip a little. Whose kids? His? She'd spent an enjoyable evening with this stranger, but he hadn't mentioned his marital status, and she hadn't asked. All she knew was that he lived with his family. What was the point of asking? She'd find out soon enough.

"Come on. You're not dressed for this weather. And by the looks of things, it'll freeze tonight. Just as well we have the tractor."

They walked to where the tractor was parked, and he helped her up. As they drove through the cold night, he pulled the tarpaulin that smelled of pine over their shoulders. "You're shivering. Move closer to me." He lifted his arm so she could get further under the tarpaulin. She did, and the heat which emanated from his body, soothed her shivers until she felt she was melting into his arms. He smelled of wholesome male outdoors—pine trees, fresh air and warm wool—and she closed her eyes and wanted the moment never to end.

"Don't go to sleep on me," he rumbled. "We're here."

She sat up, blinking under the bright snowy light. At the end of a farm track only five minutes from the town, but already deep into the countryside, was a two-story stone farmhouse from which lights spilled out across the snow, revealing neat, fenced enclosures and out-buildings. It looked ancient, but also homely and welcoming.

Demetrio drove the tractor into the open barn, jumped down and offered his hand to Ursula.

"Are you sure no one will mind?" she asked, as she jumped to the ground.

"Of course no one will mind."

She felt strangely nervous as they walked the short distance to the farmhouse. Demetrio opened the front door to reveal a stone-flagged hallway. They hung their coats on an already cluttered old-fashioned coat stand and Demetrio turned to her with a smile. "Ready?"

She felt another flutter of nerves. What did she have to be ready for? She nodded. "Ready."

He opened the door into a large kitchen and sitting room. It had a blazing fire at one end and an Aga at the other, over which a kettle was boiling. An older man of indeterminate age was asleep in the armchair beside the fire, an Italian pointer dog at his feet.

"And what time do you call this?" a very female, and certainly not old, voice called out. A beautiful woman in her twenties came into the room, one arm full of children's toys, the other balancing a tea tray. Ursula's heart sank.

"Marianna." Demetrio kissed her on the cheek, took hold of the tea tray and placed it on the sideboard. "I'd like you to meet Ursula."

Ursula kept the smile fixed on her face. It was no

hardship; she was accustomed to hiding her thoughts and emotions, used to showing poise and an aloof exterior to cover her true feelings. It was the only way to keep safe.

"Her car broke down," he continued. "So I gave her a lift. I've invited her to stay here tonight."

"Of course. The hotels will be full all week. Welcome, Ursula."

"A pleasure to meet you, Marianna. I hope my visit isn't too inconvenient?" She looked at Demetrio, feeling almost betrayed by the closeness they'd experienced over the past few hours while, all along, his wife had been waiting for him at the farmhouse. Demetrio frowned, as if confused, and looked away. Why the hell had she trusted him? Wasn't this the kind of thing from which she'd been running? People who said one thing and did another; people she loved, who didn't love her?

"Not at all. Mama and Papa will be delighted to have more people." Marianna inclined her head to Ursula. "They seem to think my three children aren't enough."

Ursula smiled faintly. "Sounds plenty to me." *Three too many.*

"And I can assure you, it *is* plenty. Come now, and sit with Papa by the fire." Marianna smiled, looking strangely unperturbed by her husband bringing home a strange woman in the middle of the night. "Demetrio!" She peered more closely at Ursula. "Are those dog hairs Ursula is covered with? You didn't use that old dog blanket, did you?" She shook her head at his shrug. "*Dio!*" She dropped the toys into a big wicker basket.

"Papa!" Marianna kissed the top of his head. "Wake up. We have a visitor." She nudged the dog. "Bacio, move!"

The dog reluctantly moved, and the old man jumped up, instantly alert. "I was just resting my eyes."

"Sure, Papa." Demetrio also kissed him. "Sit down again, and I'll get us some drinks."

But Papa wouldn't hear of it, and after greeting Ursula, he took charge of pouring them all generous glasses of red wine. They were about to sit down when a baby began crying somewhere else in the farmhouse.

Marianna and Demetrio exchanged looks. "Sit still," said Demetrio. "I'll go."

Demetrio disappeared, and Marianna smiled at Ursula. "He's so good to me."

Ursula managed to maintain her smile and nod, in what she hoped appeared like agreement. But all she could think of was what she'd like to say to him for flirting with her while he had a gorgeous wife waiting for him at home. Instead, she turned to Papa.

"You have a beautiful home, sir."

"*Grazie*. It's been in our family for many generations. But it is too big for only Nonna and me. It needs a family."

Ursula was confused. "Don't you all live here?"

"Only Nonna and Papa," Marianna replied. "That's Mama and Papa. We call Mama 'Nonna' since the kids came along. But, yes, only they live here. Demetrio and I live in Florence. But Demetrio wants to move back to the farm."

"And you don't?"

"Oh no. It's too quiet for me, but Demetrio loves it. He'll be happy here."

"Oh, it's sad that you won't be together."

Marianna looked up. "Why?"

Ursula shrugged. "Because you seem happy together."

"Me…and Demetrio?" A broad grin spread across her face. "You think we're married?" She laughed too earthily for such a beautiful woman. "No, Ursula, he's my brother. My husband, Vincenzo, is working away from home at present. Unfortunately, some things require attention whether or not it is a holiday."

A wave of relief swept through Ursula. *Ridiculous.* She'd only known him an afternoon but somehow those moments snuggled together on the tractor, with nothing all around them but the falling snow and the piney smell of wood, made her feel close to him.

"We are the only two who are home this Christmas. My sisters are either working or with their families. We're spread all over the world. It doesn't make Nonna and Papa happy, I can tell you."

The baby's tired cries became more intermittent as the pacing on the floorboards overhead continued. Marianna sighed. "I'd better go and relieve Demetrio. Come, you're yawning, I'll show you to your room. It's already made up. Nonna lives in the hope of visitors. She'll be thrilled you're here."

They said goodnight to Papa who was damping down the fire, and went out into the stone-flagged hallway from each end of which two winding wooden staircases rose. "This way." Ursula followed Marianna up the worn staircase and raised the latch on the first door which led into a corridor away from the main house. "The extension was built above the old stables. Nonna always keeps a spare bed ready and aired for visitors." She opened the first door, and Ursula looked around the room. It was furnished with a small tester bed covered with a brightly checked duvet, and antique oak furniture. A rug added a touch of comfort and color to the dark-stained floorboards.

"It's lovely."

"There's a bathroom next door." Marianna looked around. "I hope you'll be comfortable and that the kids don't wake you. They're next door and keep unsocial hours."

Ursula couldn't remember the last time she'd stayed in a house where children were so much in evidence. "I don't mind. It'll be fun. It makes it feel more like Christmas."

Marianna held her gaze with the same eyes as Demetrio—eyes that zoomed right into her, focusing on the essentials, not the externals. It was both disarming and nerve-racking at the same time. Now she knew they were siblings, Ursula couldn't believe she'd imagined otherwise. "I'm glad you found us, Ursula. I don't like to imagine you alone in a hotel room on Christmas Eve." And neither did Ursula now. But before she could respond, Marianna had quietly closed the door and retreated down the creaky wooden stairs.

Immediately the door, whose catch had barely caught, was nudged open and Bacio, the dog, clattered into the room and jumped on the bed, eyed her suspiciously, and made himself at home on the end of the bed.

Ursula tried to lure him away, tried pulling him off but, in the end, she had to admit defeat. She climbed into bed and made herself comfortable around the snoring dog.

She lay back and looked out the low window, the curtains of which she left undrawn. Beyond the farmyard, the track led to the road, and then the valley fell away, leaving an open vista of trees and mountains, all glowing under a thick carpet of snow and starlight.

How on earth had she ended up here? Deep in the heart of the Italian countryside, deep in the heart of a family? She'd begun the day determined to avoid being near family at Christmas, and she'd ended it sharing a bed with a dog that snored, and with the faint and now intermittent sound of a tired baby's cries. How would she ever sleep?

They were her last thoughts as her eyes fluttered closed and she fell into a deep sleep, where dreams of falling snow were warmed by the memory of a man's embrace.

CHAPTER 2

rsula lay quietly under the thick duvet for a few moments as she tried to figure out where she was. Through the window, an outside light illuminated the already bright snow, making it gleam against a still dark sky.

Italy. Abbadia San Alexis. A farmhouse. She grinned to herself, and stretched out her legs either side of the dog who still refused to move. She sighed, feeling more rested than she had in a long time. It was only when she sat up in bed that she saw them—two small faces looking silently at her through the open door, silhouetted against a night light. One of the faces giggled, and the other one nudged the giggling one, who promptly stopped. *Ah, Marianna's kids.*

She reached over and turned on the side light, revealing a girl aged about seven and a younger boy, more solemn, sucking his thumb as he frowned at her. A knitted toy of obscure origins was threaded between his fingers.

"*Ciao*! You're up early." Ursula roughly combed her hair with her fingers.

There was another giggle from the girl. "We're always up early. Mama told us to go away and not come back until at least six."

"And what time is it now?" Ursula looked at her phone. "Ah, five-thirty." She tried to recall the last time she'd seen five-thirty in the morning. Probably an international flight. It certainly wasn't a time of day with which she was familiar. She propped herself up on an elbow and smiled at the two faces—one cheeky, a giggle ready at any moment, and the other, serious. "So are you coming in or are you going to get cold staring at me from the landing?"

The girl pushed the boy, and they scampered inside and across the colorful rug which was spread on the thick planks of darkened oak. The boy continued to suck his thumb as he peered at her with intense and curious eyes. A silent shiver racked through his small frame.

Ursula shifted over on the bed and patted the space she'd vacated. "Come and get under the covers."

"Your name is Orsula." The little girl said as she tugged her brother to climb up next to her on the bed, but not where Ursula had left a space, but at the other end where the dog still lay sleeping.

Ursula was thankful she'd put on her pajamas as the boy and girl wriggled under the duvet, their cold feet meeting her warm ones. They gazed at her while they patted the oblivious dog, who continued to snore.

"That's right. Orsula is the Italian for Ursula. And what are your names?"

"This is Tomasso." The girl poked the boy in the ribs,

but he didn't react. He was obviously used to it. "And I'm Carolina."

"Pleased to meet you, Carolina and Tomasso."

"Mama says Orsula means 'little bear.' Are you fierce like a bear?"

Ursula laughed and then let the laughter die as she pondered the child's question. She couldn't remember the last time she'd lost her temper. She always managed to suppress her irritation or anger, to move on, to move away, before it could surface. "No, I'm not fierce."

"Then you're cuddly like my toy bear?"

She raised her eyebrows in surprise at the inquisition and tried to recall the last time she'd cuddled someone, without it being a prelude to sex. She couldn't. "Not so sure I'm cuddly either."

"Then what are you?"

"Somewhere in between, I suspect."

Carolina frowned and at that moment, Ursula could see the striking similarity between brother and sister. But, with the sister, the frown was short-lived. "Sort of like someone is when they're waiting for something, then."

Ursula gave a quick smile to hide her surprise. Tomasso continued to stare at her, a slight frown on his face, while he sucked his thumb. Carolina looked around the room, ignorant of the fact that she'd just revealed something to Ursula of which she'd been completely unaware. "Probably. Anyway, let's talk about you. Do you always wander into stranger's rooms?"

"No. But Mama said she liked you so we thought it would be all right." Carolina pointed to Ursula's sponge bag. "That's pretty."

"Would you like to see inside?"

Carolina twisted her mouth as she tried to repress an excited smile. "*Si!*"

Ursula lay it on top of the duvet and unzipped it. Carolina crawled across the covers, her eyes huge, as Ursula took out the expensive bottles and lotions and miscellaneous other things she'd accumulated that required such a large bag. Carolina fingered a small cut-glass bottle of perfume. It was a delicate pink with a gold top.

"Would you like to try some?"

She nodded, seemingly overcome by being allowed to look at such exquisite treasures. Ursula sprayed some perfume on Carolina's upturned wrist.

"Um, it's lovely."

"You can have it if you like."

"Really?"

"Sure." She looked at the silent boy, who'd emerged from the other end of the bed to climb in beside her. "And Tomasso, is there anything you'd like?"

"Oh, all Tomasso ever wants is a story," Carolina said dismissively.

"A story, hey? Well, let me think. How about a story about a Swedish boy who is turned into a *tomte*—which is like a little gnome or pixie—and jumps on the back of a goose and flies over Sweden?"

Tomasso's eyes widened, and he nodded vigorously.

Ursula told the story as Carolina fingered through Ursula's trinkets until she yawned, also snuggled in close to Ursula, and went to sleep. Tomasso continued to listen until he, too, eventually fell asleep. With both the children and the dog fast asleep, Ursula lay back, closed her eyes, and joined them.

It wasn't until much later, when early morning sunshine flooded the room that Ursula awoke to discover they'd all gone.

URSULA OPENED the door to the kitchen, and a wall of heat and noise hit her. A woman in her sixties sat at the table and noticed Ursula immediately. Her mouth turned into a perfect O-shape. "Demetrio! You didn't tell me she's beautiful."

Demetrio grinned at Ursula, and dragged out an oak-backed chair with a rush seat for her. "Because you didn't ask."

Ursula reached across the table to the woman and shook her hand. "A pleasure to meet you, Signora Pecora. Thank you so much for letting me stay the night."

The woman dismissed her thanks with a wave of her hand. "We wouldn't have a stranger left to find a room on such a night." The woman called out to her husband who was just entering the room. "Papa! Come and meet Orsula."

Papa tipped his cap at Ursula. "We've met already. Last night."

"You men! You tell me nothing."

Papa merely smiled, plainly used to this admonishment, before disappearing outside again, toward the sound of children's laughter.

"Come, Orsula," continued Nonna. "Sit beside me so I can see you better."

Ursula did as she was told, and Marianna slipped a cup of coffee onto the table in front of her. "I hope you slept well?"

"Of course she slept well, Marianna! Why wouldn't she?" interjected Nonna.

Demetrio laughed as he brought *fette biscottate* and warm rolls fresh from the oven, to the table. "Nonna is very superstitious. She believes that only if you are in the wrong place, at the wrong time, will you not be able to sleep."

"Then, I'm in the right place at the right time."

Demetrio looked up and held Ursula's gaze. His eyes were warm and a slight smile played on his lips. "*Si*, I believe you are."

Ursula looked down at her coffee and took a studied sip, trying her best to ignore his gaze that played such havoc with her senses.

Marianna looked from one to the other of them, and grinned. Then she saw Ursula's confusion and changed the subject. "In the wrong place if you ask me. Too close to the kids' bedrooms. I hear you had an early morning visit from two of my brood." She grimaced. "Sorry about that."

"No problem. They're adorable."

Marianna frowned playfully. "Are you sure you're talking about my kids?"

"A giggling girl, and a boy who loves stories?"

"They're the ones!"

As if on cue, the two children she'd met earlier entered the room, followed by a weary-looking Papa carrying a wriggling baby in his arms.

Nonna opened her arms wide. "Children, come here and tell me what you've been doing." She picked up a wet cloth, and while Tomasso tried to describe the books Papa had been showing them, she wiped the ring of milk from around his mouth, before beckoning for Marianna to rinse the cloth through. She did so immediately. There was no doubt as to who was in charge of *this* household.

By turns, Nonna petted her grandchildren and organized her children. She gave instructions to Marianna on how hot the milk should be for the *caffè latte*, while simultaneously admonishing Demetrio for allowing Ursula to be covered by the dog blanket, and heaping food onto her husband's plate. Papa sat quietly, only glancing up from time to time, to beam benignly on everyone.

After what seemed to Ursula to be a chaotic quarter hour, everyone was seated around the scrubbed pine table, even the little ones, and tucking into their plates of warm bread rolls, butter, jam, cookies and leftover mini frittatas covered with spicy tomato sauce. But even then, the talk didn't die down. Between mouthfuls of food, each of the family had something to say.

"Vincenzo called," Marianna said. "Would you believe he has to work over Christmas?"

"Noooo!" said Nonna in equally shocked tones. "But why?"

Marianna turned to Ursula. "As I mentioned before, Vincenzo is my husband, and his company works him too hard. He was meant to be joining us in a few days." She turned back to her mother. "He says he can't leave Budapest until the contract is signed and sealed."

"Then why don't you go to him? The children will be fine with me here." Nonna turned to the little ones. "Won't you, *tesori mio?*"

Carolina's smile revealed her missing baby teeth. Tomasso nodded, but his frown didn't disappear. Ursula was beginning to wonder why he frowned so much.

"There! You see. Go to your husband. A man needs his woman beside him at Christmas."

"Nonna!" Marianna screwed up her face and shook her head. "You're living in the dark ages. Vincenzo is fine. He's on his own, in a flash hotel, food whenever he likes."

"Fine? You think living in a hotel is fine? No!" Nonna shook her head fiercely. "*No*, Marianna. A man needs his home and family around him. Especially at Christmas." She leaned over and grasped Papa's hand who looked up, startled. "Isn't that so, Papa? Remember the time when I was in hospital with Demetrio?" Papa nodded and turned his attention back to the frittata. Nonna addressed Ursula. "It was a difficult birth. Demetrio was so big, and my midwife insisted we go to hospital. But"—she shrugged—"it was fine in the end." She grinned at Demetrio. "And I got myself a big, bouncing boy." She blew a kiss across the table to Demetrio, who rolled his eyes and took her hand and kissed it with exaggerated courtesy. Then she leaned into Ursula. "A big bouncing boy who I still worry about."

"Nonna!" Demetrio exclaimed. "I left home over ten years ago. There's no need to worry about me. I have my own business—"

"Business? What kind of business is landscape design?"

"I thought you were a farmer," Ursula said, surprised.

"He *should* be a farmer," Nonna said triumphantly, turning back to Demetrio. "The farm is *here*, Demetrio. Your father isn't getting any younger."

"Nonna!" said Papa, indignation stirring him from his breakfast. "I *think* I can manage my own farm."

Nonna shrugged. "You may think so…" She shrugged again, conveying her doubt in that one gesture.

Demetrio shook his head and turned to Ursula. "I have

a landscaping business which despite what Nonna infers—"

"I'm not inferring anything! I'm *saying* that you should be *here*, on the farm, where you belong—"

"In spite of what Nonna *says*, I'm more than happy in my work, and I have a great team of people working for me."

"And you're based in Florence?" asked Ursula.

"Yes. But of course, my work takes me all over Italy."

"What kind of landscaping do you do?"

"I specialize in sustainable landscaping—landscaping with heritage in mind—preserving the past for the future. That's why I enjoy coming home so much."

"Of course you do. Because it *is* your home, Demetrio," said Nonna.

Demetrio ignored his mother's interruption. "As I was saying, I enjoy coming home—aside from the wonderful company—because this land has been untouched for centuries, and I'd have it remain so."

"Then you should come home and help your Papa with the land!"

"Nonna! I have another home, another life, in Florence." He took hold of her hand and squeezed it. "Of course this is my family home, but I'm happy with my life. Why do you worry about me?"

Nonna shrugged and continued to eat, knowing full well she had the attention of everyone. "You've not been truly happy since Elisabetta died."

The clatter of forks on dishes and conversation immediately stopped, and there was absolute silence. Ursula looked up at Demetrio in time to see his face fall and his eyes cloud over with pain. She looked away, not wanting him to know she'd witnessed his look of devastation.

Papa leaned over to Nonna and placed a worn, weathered hand on hers. "Nonna," he said reproachfully.

She shrugged. "Well… I don't know… it's just…" But she must have realized the pain she'd caused because she put another frittata on Demetrio's plate, poured him some more coffee and pushed his mug toward him as if food and a hot drink would cure everything.

Ursula helped the baby, Lorenzo, fill his spoon with yoghurt which he then decided to hurl across the table at Carolina who shrieked and burst into noisy tears.

Marianna leaped up, obviously relieved to break the silence and wiped Carolina's face. She gave a hug to console her, while Lorenzo stolidly picked up Tomasso's spoon and began feeding himself, apparently oblivious to, or maybe *happy* because of, the chaos he'd created.

Ursula wiped up the mess, not wanting Demetrio to be aware that she'd witnessed the breach in his defenses, not wanting him to know that she'd seen the pain that lay beneath that happy and charming exterior.

No doubt about it—Demetrio had loved and lost. But not lost in the sense of being rejected, lost as in completely and irrevocably. Ursula's heart went out to him, but all she could do was give him space, by helping Marianna and the children clear up the breakfast things, and allow him time to recover.

By the time Ursula returned to the table with a fresh jug of coffee, things seemed to have returned to normal. Demetrio was sitting facing Tomasso, with one arm casually slung over the back of the chair, while he told a rapt audience about a local tale of legendary animals that were sighted in the woods every Christmas. Tomasso's eyes were wide, and the frown had disappeared.

Marianna brought another warm roll from the oven for Papa, who, despite his slender build, appeared to eat more than anyone else. "Demetrio! Don't fill Tomasso's head with all that superstitious nonsense!"

Demetrio ruffled the boy's hair. "He can cope. Can't you Tomasso?"

Tomasso nodded, wide-eyed. "Of course I can. And it's true, Mama, Uncle says it is."

Marianna shook her head at Demetrio and returned to the kitchen. Demetrio cleared his throat and changed the subject. "So, Ursula, do you have any plans today? No"—he held up his hand with a grin—"I nearly forgot. You don't plan, do you?"

"I plan 99.9% of the time. My friends and family wouldn't understand how I came to be here, in the holiday season, without accommodation booked. They'd think something strange has happened."

Demetrio didn't miss a beat. "Has it?"

Ursula suddenly realized they were virtually alone—Papa had taken their empty plates to the kitchen sink and was talking to Marianna about her husband's work, and Carolina and Tomasso had slid under the table and were surreptitiously feeding the dog. Nonna's attention, meanwhile, was focused on trying to wipe Lorenzo's face.

"Has it?" Demetrio repeated. They looked at each other across the stained and worn pine table with the remnants of breakfast cups, bread crumbs, all the ordinary things of life, with a gaze that was most definitely *not* ordinary. "Maybe," she said softly. She shrugged. "I don't know yet."

Demetrio sat back in his chair and smiled—a confident, warm, kind and inviting smile. She could have given a list of adjectives to describe that smile, but she didn't need to dissect it to understand it. She felt it from the tips of her toes, up through her body, through to her fingers, which she flexed, as she tried to prevent herself from responding.

He leaned forward, resting his folded arms on the table, his gaze suddenly more intense. "When will you know?"

She sucked in a deep breath as she tried to control the shimmer of need that went through her body. Nonna, now freed from Lorenzo by Marianna, saved Ursula from replying by commanding attention once more.

Nonna turned to Demetrio and slapped his arms. "Not on the table. I've brought you up better than that!" He shook his head and laughed. "So," she continued. "You'll be going into Abbadia today to finish off the preparations for tonight?"

"Of course," Demetrio replied. "I've been doing it for over ten years. I'm not going to stop now." He stood up and looked down at Ursula. "Would you like to come along and watch?"

"I'd like to come along and help if I can. And I need to check out accommodation."

Nonna's face dropped. "But there's no need. You can stay here, with us."

"But I can't impose on your family at Christmas."

"You're not imposing. I like having guests. Besides, there won't be any free rooms at the hotels. People stay for the week of festivals, not for only one night."

Demetrio shook his head. "Nonna's right. There won't

be any rooms available. I'm afraid you're stuck with us, unless you wish to drive back to Florence tonight, of course. But you won't be doing that, I hope?"

The "I hope" caught her off guard and, by the look on his face, it had caught him off guard too. He grinned and looked away as if surprised at what he'd said.

"I won't leave if you're okay for me to stay another night. I'd intended to go to Florence in a few days. I've made arrangements to see a friend there in the New Year."

"Good," Marianna chipped in. "It'll give you a chance to see Abbadia at its most festive. Now go, you two. Get to work. We expect a good show tonight!"

"Let me clear up first," said Ursula.

But Marianna wouldn't hear of it. She was exactly like her mother—a matriarch-in-waiting, and utterly in control.

Demetrio lifted the crocheted blanket which covered Nonna's lap, and Ursula noticed what she'd failed to see before, Nonna was in a wheelchair. Demetrio pushed her over to the fire. He gave her a cup of coffee, and then she shooed him away.

"You go, Demetrio. Take Orsula and show her what Abbadia has to offer."

"I'll have to arrange to get my car towed back first," said Ursula.

Demetrio picked up the keys to the Land Rover. "As if I'd let you pay a lot of money for some garage hand in town to do that, even if you *could* find one. Let's go and get it now, while it's not snowing."

"Are you sure I'm not keeping you from anything?" Ursula asked, as they walked into the hallway.

"Nothing that can't wait."

"I feel terrible. You've done so much for me already. I'm in your debt."

"Um." Demetrio grinned as he took his coat off the peg. "I think I'll need that debt repaying today."

The gleam in his eye made her blush. "Really?"

"Yes, really." He looked her up and down. From her soft leather boots, up her stylish gray trousers, to her black top. "Do you have any practical clothes in that Gucci suitcase of yours?"

"Yes, of course! I have a pair of… jeans." Probably best not to mention the designer brand. "And a… sweater." Not that she'd ever actually referred to her angora top as a sweater.

"Good. Any woolly hats, scarfs, gloves?"

"No! Of course not. I haven't worn a woolly hat since I was a school girl."

"Time to start. Marianna will lend you what you need."

"So… my debt is to be paid by going somewhere cold."

"Yes. And then working your butt off."

"Outside, on the land?" Ursula pulled a nervous face. "Not exactly my forte but I'll give it a go."

"Good girl!" He pulled his hat from the hat stand. "Now let's go and dig your car out."

Ursula had thought Demetrio's comment about "digging the car out" was a turn of phrase. But after they reached the place where it was parked, she realized that "digging" was *precisely* what he'd meant. She stepped out of the Land Rover and looked in despair at the car, now just a mound of snow, bright in the early morning sunlight.

Demetrio looked up at the sky. "At least we have the sun on our side. It's melting the snow, which will make our job easier." He grabbed a couple of spades from the back of the Land Rover and began shoveling snow from around the base of the car.

He was right about the sun. With its help the car was soon exposed, and when Ursula stood back she was out of breath and hot under the borrowed clothes and sunshine. The place was as lovely as she remembered from the day before, with the trees rising out of the valley below, laden with snow. There was little traffic on the road, and the valley was still and quiet.

"It's so beautiful here," Ursula said.

"Yes, it's very special."

"It looks untouched."

"Virtually. Papa has had to do some work on it, but it was purely restorative."

"This is *your* land? But it's miles from the farm."

"The farm is part of a much larger estate. If you think this is beautiful, come over the fence, and I'll show you something even more spectacular."

He leaped over the fence, and held out a hand for her. She took it and climbed over. The snow was less thick on the sheltered side of the valley, and they managed to follow the path that wound below the road, toward the place where the steep slopes met.

Ursula stopped suddenly. "The air. It feels different here. Colder somehow."

"Look down there." Demetrio moved aside so she could see better.

Ursula gasped. She couldn't believe what she was seeing. The section of the hillside they were looking at was devoid of trees. Down the center of a rock face, where water normally flowed, was a sheet of frozen ice, framed by icicles. "I've never seen such a thing! Is it a frozen waterfall?"

"*Si*. It's amazing, isn't it? It's one of my favorite places."

"Is it frozen solid?"

"Yes, for a short time. As a kid I used to think it was as if someone from a fairy tale had stumbled into the woods and touched the water, turning it to ice. Probably my grandmother spun me some old tale."

"That's so different to my upbringing. In Sweden, there was ice all around, and I knew all about how water molecules slowed down and stuck together as the temperature freezes. No magic, only science."

"And in Italy? There is no science, only magic."

She laughed. "Of course."

"And in summer the water is magically warmed, and we swim in the plunge pool below. It's fun taking Marianna's kids there now." He leaned against a tree. "As I get older I begin to understand how my father feels about this place, and his father before him. There's something in the blood, a need to make sure it's here for my children."

Ursula glanced at him and then turned away, trying to collect her thoughts. "You didn't mention your children before."

"That's because I don't have any. Not yet. But of course, I hope to. Doesn't everyone?"

"No. Neither my sister or brother have children. Both are married, but neither show any interest in children."

"And you?"

She shrugged. "I don't know. I was in a relationship for a few years, and I thought we might marry and have children. But it wasn't to be." And before her ex, there was Alessandro. The thought of him, married now, with a child, was like the twist of a knife in a wound that refused to heal. She blinked lightly and smiled, turning back to Demetrio, to find him closer, watching her. "But, that's okay. These things happen."

"Yes, they do. As you no doubt realize from what my mother said, I was married. My wife died."

"I'm sorry. How long ago?"

"Just over two years now. It's taken me this long to believe my family when they tell me that life goes on." He took hold of her hand again. "I'm beginning to think they're right, after all. I find I'm looking at things—the land around us, people, you—and finding myself unexpectedly happy again."

Ursula swallowed and tried to contain yet another blush. "So… can we get closer to the waterfall?"

"Sure. And I'll show you something that will make you believe in magic."

She smiled, shaking her head. "Before I did my law degree I studied science. I don't believe in magic. I believe in what can be proven by science."

He sighed and shook his head. "We'll see about that. Walk this way, Ms. Adamsson." He held out his hand as if laying down a challenge, and she took it and he curled his gloved hand around hers. "Got to hold on tight," he said, explaining his tight grip. "And watch where you put your feet." He grinned. "Just as well Marianna lent you her boots."

As well as the thermal underwear, Ursula thought.

They walked carefully toward the frozen waterfall—its long, sleek plumes of water hard and unreal. At that moment, the sun rose over the hillside casting its bright light onto the ruffled sheets of ice. Ursula had never seen anything as beautiful—not in her native Sweden, nor in any of the cosmopolitan cities in which she spent most of her life. "It's stunning."

She turned to him and met his gaze. "Stunning," he repeated. But he wasn't looking at the frozen waterfall, only her. She suddenly felt self-conscious and pulled the soft gray hat that Marianna had lent her, lower over her blonde hair. She smiled uncertainly. "Come on," he continued. "I can see you're still not persuaded about the magic."

He walked carefully along the ledge which ran between the sheet of ice and the rock face. Ursula felt a flutter of nerves but was urged on by the warm, confident grip of his hand. She stepped behind the curtain of ice, and was robbed of breath.

The sheet of ice was aqua blue from behind. She reached out to touch it, but his grip on her other hand tightened, warning her not to move. She withdrew her outstretched hand. She didn't need to touch it to appreciate it. "You're right. It *is* magic." At that moment, a stray beam of sunlight penetrated the ice and illuminated the mossy green of the wall behind, splitting the light into a rainbow of colors.

Inexplicably Ursula felt tears prick her eyes. What was going on? She never cried. She turned away so he couldn't see her expression because she was afraid her defenses were blown. She sucked in the icy cold air, its frigid temperature searing her lungs and drying the tears. She turned and smiled. "Magic," she repeated.

With his eyes never leaving hers, he lifted her chin with his finger and kissed her, light as a feather, on her mouth. His finger swept her jaw before he stepped away. "I'm sorry. You looked irresistible with the word 'magic' still lingering on your lips."

She looked away, confused. Another thing she rarely felt.

"We should be getting back," he said, as if reading her mind. "Nonna will be giving Papa a hard time, no doubt suggesting they call out a search party. For my father's sake, we should return."

"And for my sake, also, Demetrio. I'm beginning to wonder whether too much magic in one day may be detrimental to a woman's rational mind."

"Maybe. But surely that's a small price to pay for happiness?"

They walked in silence up the hill—still hand in hand, despite the fact there was no danger now they were away from the rock face—and up onto the road. Within minutes Demetrio had jump-started the car and, with snow-chains fitted, Ursula followed Demetrio in the Land Rover back to the farm, her thoughts on the man outlined in the driver's seat, who looked, too frequently, through his rear vision window at her, a smile in his eyes.

CHAPTER 3

$\mathcal{B}$y the time they reached the farmhouse, it was late morning, and delicious smells drifted out from the steamy kitchen's open window.

As they walked up to the house, Ursula felt a moment of regret that they were about to enter family life again. All she wanted to do was go somewhere quiet and get to know Demetrio better. That he was gorgeous, she'd known straight away. But that he was also such a nice person? She hadn't dared to hope. But with each passing hour, as he'd interacted with her, and his family, his personality had unfolded, confirming her hopes and more. He wasn't only kind and loving, but also strong and dependable—traits she'd never imagined seeing all together in one man. She felt as if she knew him. And then there was that kiss. Well, that was like the full stop at the end of a cliff-hanger sentence—inevitable, but leaving you wanting more.

But, she reminded herself, there was no point in

wanting more. She was leaving the day after Christmas Day and would never see him again. That's the way it went in her world. After all, hadn't she'd come here with the express aim of getting away from families? They weren't for her. Life had made that clear. No, she wouldn't be spending any more alone time with Demetrio if she could help it. There was no point.

But still. Ursula watched as Demetrio pulled off his hat, revealing his long, gorgeous dark curls. He smiled as he stepped back, allowing her to ascend the steps to the front door before him. The way he looked at her, with interest and appreciation, was downright seductive. And that kiss. Again, that kiss. Desire tugged at her deep inside just thinking about it.

Demetrio opened the front door and had stepped aside for Ursula to enter, when Carolina and Tomasso came running out and leaped into Demetrio's arms. Demetrio followed Ursula inside, with one child hanging off each arm. In the kitchen, preparations were already well underway for dinner that night.

"Ursula!" greeted Marianna. "Come and sit down. Would you like a coffee?"

"A coffee would be wonderful but can I help you?"

Marianna turned to her with a flushed face, hot from the Aga as she basted the meat. "Have a hot drink first; you must be freezing. Everything all right with your car?"

"After we dug it out of the snow drift, Demetrio jump-started it, and he's going to check the ignition later."

Marianna passed Ursula a steaming cup of black coffee and a plate of warm biscuits. "Straight from the oven." Marianna grinned. "Nonna keeps me busy while I'm here."

"I feel guilty. You're doing all the work."

"Here, you can help with this if you like." Ursula was about to ask what it was and then realized it wouldn't make any difference, she knew nothing about cooking.

"I'm afraid I'm a willing, but not very good, cook."

"You don't have to be good." She indicated a saucepan over a low heat with some kind of lumpy mixture in the middle and handed Ursula a jug of milk. "You simply need to know how to handle a wooden spoon."

"Sure." Ursula frowned, hoping she wouldn't prove to be the first person in history who didn't know how to handle a wooden spoon. She didn't want to admit she'd never done such a task before. Outside her usual life, her lack of experience looked ridiculous.

Demetrio had followed Ursula and tried to release Carolina and Tomasso as they entered the kitchen, but they continued to cling to his arms. They laughed as Demetrio lifted them as if they didn't weigh a thing.

"Carolina! Tomasso! Let go of your uncle."

"Where are they?" Demetrio said, twisting around, pretending to be unaware of the two children who dangled from his arms. "I don't see them. I'll go and try to find out where they are." With the children swinging on his arms, he turned and walked back out into the hallway, the children screaming with laughter.

"My brother dotes on those kids."

"It looks as if it's reciprocated."

"Oh yes. They adore him." Marianna looked up with a grin. "Demetrio is their favorite uncle. And their favorite aunty was Elisabetta—" Marianna stopped suddenly.

"Elisabetta. Ah, your mother mentioned her last night. She was Demetrio's wife, right?"

"Yes, I'm sorry, my tongue runs away with me. Demetrio's no doubt told you about her?"

"A little."

"She died several years ago now, but the kids have never forgotten her. Especially Carolina. She adored her."

Ursula fixed a polite smile on her face, determined to hide the plunging feeling in her gut at hearing the name of Demetrio's wife. *Ridiculous*, she told herself firmly.

"Was it sudden?"

"An undiagnosed heart problem. She died in Demetrio's arms." Marianna dropped a ladle into the sink with a clatter and gripped the sides of the wooden bench. "I'm sorry. It's still hard. Especially for Demetrio." She took a deep breath and smiled bravely at Ursula. "Let's change the subject. You're here, and it's Christmas and I want everyone to be happy."

"Of course," said Ursula with an answering smile. "So, what is it you're cooking?" She continued to stir the floury mixture which remained a lump, as she peered into the oven pan in which Marianna was basting some meat.

"Ragu, eventually. We slow cook the meat today for tomorrow's Christmas dinner. And tonight's pasta and seafood are already prepared. I use Nonna's recipe for tomorrow's dinner but we're having something a little different tonight. Not the usual dishes, you know."

Ursula didn't know. She owned no recipe books and had never seen anything like the handwritten volume to which Marianna was referring.

"This," Marianna said, smoothing her hand over the big black book from which pieces of paper projected, "is our family bible. We all add notes and recipes to it."

Ursula peered at it. "It's a wonder you can follow it."

"Certainly my handwriting!" Marianna said, indicating a particularly bold scrawl.

Ursula pointed to frequent additions in neat capital letters. "Whoever wrote this seemed to know what they were doing."

"Ah." Marianna said. "That was Elisabetta."

Ursula's heart sank. She had the distinct feeling that Elisabetta was never going to be far from everyone's heart and minds.

"She knew all there was to know about cooking," continued Marianna. "She was a brilliant chef and would have been a brilliant mother. She loved children."

Ursula shook her head, conflicted by her sadness that Demetrio should have had such a tragedy in his life, and that this woman was far more suited to him, to his family and lifestyle, than she could ever be. She picked up the plastic bowl, which Lorenzo had thrown onto the ground for the third time.

Marianna grinned. "You're good with kids."

Ursula grunted. "I don't think so. I've zero experience with them. But Carolina and Tomasso are adorable. And so is little Lorenzo."

"They're good kids. They miss their father." Marianna's smile dropped for a moment. "But we can't do anything about that. Vincenzo is working hard, and he has to. He'll be home soon though."

"Good, because I'm sure he's missing you all, as much as you're missing him." She turned to see Demetrio dangling both children by their ankles as they screamed with laughter. "But at least they have their uncle here."

"Yes. Demetrio is a much-loved uncle all right. I just wish he'd hurry up and have children of his own."

Ursula looked away from Marianna's thoughtful gaze. "Perhaps he doesn't want children."

"He wants children all right. It's his past he doesn't want to leave behind."

"Total opposite to me, then."

Marianna popped the meat back in the oven and began working on some fish. "How so?"

"I'm quite happy to move on, to leave my past behind. And I won't be having children."

"Really?" Marianna stopped what she was doing and stared at Ursula in disbelief. "Why's that?"

"I hated my childhood. I was brought up by my grandmother when my parents split up. My mother went to live in Antigua with a wealthy man whose plans certainly didn't include a child that wasn't his, and my father's work had him constantly traveling around the world. I have two full siblings who are much older than me, who weren't so affected by my parent's divorce. But I was lonely and I'm all too aware of the tragedy of bringing a child into the world on a whim. There will be no whims for me."

"That's fair enough, but maybe you'll change your mind when you meet the right man."

"I can't see that happening. No, I'll never have kids. And that's fine with me."

There was a scrape of a chair close by and Marianna and Ursula both turned to see Demetrio pushing his mother's wheelchair into place under the scrubbed pine table. He frowned as he helped his mother with something. Ursula had no idea whether he'd heard her or not. "Smells good," he said.

Marianna turned around to stir the sauce for the

tortellini which was beginning to catch. "Salt cod, eel, and tortellini."

"A feast, as usual."

"Uncle!" shouted Carolina from the other room.

"Excuse me, my tyrants call." He walked back into the hall where the children were hiding, very ineptly.

"Feast!" Nonna repeated grumpily. "We had plain pasta growing up. Nothing fancy like these southern fish dishes."

"Oh, Nonna! You know you enjoy them," said Marianna.

Nonna leaned across the table and began preparing vegetables. "In my day Christmas Eve was a time for fasting. I like *tradition*."

Marianna shared a conspiratorial grin with Ursula. "And we like tradition, too, Nonna. First, we have the procession with the torches through the street and the lighting of the fire. And then, although there is food in the square, we will eat back here before we go to Midnight Mass."

Church? Ursula couldn't remember the last time she'd gone to church with the aim of participating, rather than appreciating its architecture and art.

Marianna reached over and gave the contents of Ursula's saucepan a stir and pushed the milk towards her, nodded encouragingly for Ursula to blend the two. Ursula sloshed in the liquid and immediately splashed herself with the first turn of the wooden spoon. Marianna passed her an apron.

"Tradition is what I like," Nonna repeated as if nothing had been said. She looked peevishly out to the hall from where shouts of the children and Demetrio could be heard. "I wish Demetrio was more interested in tradition."

"How can you say that, Nonna? You know how much he cares about this place."

Nonna shrugged. "You know what I mean."

Marianna shot her a quick, perceptive glance. "Are you in pain, Nonna?"

The old lady waved an irritated hand. "No more than usual." But Ursula suddenly noticed the tell-tale creasing of lines around her eyes and the pinched look around her mouth. "Papa's gone into town, to get me more medication. I'll be fine. It's Demetrio, I worry about. He should have children of his own."

"Nonna!" Marianna exclaimed as she saw Demetrio standing in the kitchen door, having stopped abruptly as he heard his mother's last words. But Nonna had her back to the door.

"Demetrio's waited long enough. Elisabetta's been dead these two years."

Ursula watched the fun drain from Demetrio's face as the children slipped away quietly, aware of the sudden change in atmosphere.

"I didn't realize there was a set time for mourning," he said.

Nonna turned suddenly. "I'm just worried about you, Demetrio. I want to see you happy and settled."

"Nonna's not feeling well, Demetrio," Marianna interjected, trying to calm things.

Demetrio smiled reassuringly at Marianna before dropping a kiss on his mother's head. "Has Papa gone for more medicine?"

"Yes," replied Nonna. "But it's you I'm worried about."

He drew in a deep breath. "Thank you for your concern, but I can assure you I'm fine."

"You'll be *more* fine with children."

"Maybe. But children aren't something one can pluck out of thin air, not something I can conjure up with a click of my fingers. If, and when, the time is right, then of course I'll have children."

Nonna sighed, and patted his hand. "You're a good boy, my son. I just want the best for you. I don't understand these modern ways. In my day we courted, married and had children. Life was simple."

The turn of the conversation was making Ursula nervous, and she focused on the saucepan before her, in which the solid mass remained unaffected by the pool of milk which was beginning to bubble around it. She prodded it with the spoon. Somehow she doubted it should look like that. How did you get two such disparate things to blend? Wasn't that what electric mixers were for? Or, more to the point, wasn't that what bakeries were for?

"Orsula, don't you think Demetrio would make a good father?" Nonna cast her bespectacled gaze on Ursula. Demetrio rolled his eyes in exasperation.

"Nonna!" remonstrated Marianna.

Ursula didn't like the way this conversation was progressing. She swallowed. She hadn't felt this nervous since ninth grade when she'd been caught shopping when she should have been at school. "From what I've seen, yes, of course," she said, hoping that would end the conversation. She turned quickly back to the saucepan whose ingredients were no closer to amalgamating than when she'd started.

"And do you want children, Ursula?"

"Nonna!" Demetrio and Marianna exclaimed in unison.

Ursula's heart beat fast, but honesty was important to her. She was a cuckoo in this family's nest, an interloper, someone who couldn't cook, and who had no intention of ever having children.

She shook her head. "No." She smiled regretfully at Demetrio and Marianna. "I'm not planning to have children."

If the hush had been awkward up till that point, it was even more so now. Ursula glanced from one to the other of them, their faces holding a mixture of surprise and disbelief. All except Demetrio, who looked sad. He blinked and looked away.

"Enough of the interrogation," Demetrio said, as he poured his mother a cup of coffee and placed it on the table in front of her. "Ursula is a guest here, and her plans are none of your… or *our* business."

Marianna mouthed "sorry" to her. But it didn't make her feel any better. Demetrio's use of the word "our" made Ursula feel suddenly empty. She stopped stirring. By using the word "our," he'd accepted the barrier which she'd placed between them. He plainly wanted children, and she didn't. Family was important to him, and it wasn't to her. She tried to swallow down the lump that had risen from nowhere. But it refused to budge—much like the lump at the bottom of the saucepan. The gas flame licked around the base of the pan.

"Is that burning I can smell?" Nonna wheeled herself to the stove, and Ursula stepped away as Marianna rushed over and took the pan off the heat. They both looked at Ursula who stepped back toward the door.

"Sorry, I—"

Just then Papa entered the room, whistling under his breath. His eyes darted from one to the other before he poured a glass of water, and put the medicine in front of his wife. "Adela, here's your medicine." He sat down. "Ursula, come sit beside me and talk to an old man."

But she couldn't. "I'm sorry. If you don't mind, I think I'll just step outside for some fresh air."

"Of course," Marianna exclaimed, too heartily. "The path through the farmyard takes you to the top of the ridge. There's a lovely view from up there."

Ursula didn't need telling twice and, without looking around, she went into the hall, donned the oversized gray sweater, hat and scarf she'd borrowed from Marianna, and slipped outside into the freezing air. The cold air burned her lungs, and slowed the urgent beating of her heart which thudded like a warning that, as amazing as this world was, it wasn't hers and would never be.

She walked past the farm buildings, pushed open the gate that Marianna had indicated and walked quickly along the forest path, hardly aware of the beauty of the white landscape, just needing to put distance between herself and that alien world that could never be hers.

Puffed with exertion, she reached the top of the hill and looked around. Hands on hips she regained her breath as she marveled at the beauty all around her—from the ancient chestnut trees to the mountain that rose up beyond them. The light had changed from the brilliance of early morning and a hazy mist now muted the contours of the land.

"Beautiful, isn't it?"

She jumped around. "Demetrio! I didn't realize—"

"That I was following you?" He grinned and walked up beside her. "Of course I was. My mother was worried she'd upset you. My mother wouldn't usually say such things. But she's not well, and she appears to be worried about me." He shrugged. "Why, I don't know. And so she said things she'd never normally say."

Ursula shrugged. "She was only speaking her mind." It was her turn to smile. "I'm not used to that."

"It's not always a good thing. But she *is* sorry, so I hope you won't hold it against her."

"Of course not. Your mother has made me most welcome and has been so kind. But…"

"But she's from a different world. Tradition is everything to her. And, although she doesn't seem to believe me, it's everything to me, too. The older I get, the more I realize it. Take these woods. We've had offers for this land, but Papa has always refused them. And, when I inherit, I'll continue to refuse them."

"What do they want to do with it?"

"One company wanted to build luxury cabins in the woods. Another company wanted the trees for logging." He slapped the trunk of a tree, stroking his hand against its rough bark as though it were the most luxurious fabric. "But they're not going anywhere."

As Demetrio gazed around his white world, Ursula was aware that she was in the presence of an emotionally fulfilled man. He may have loved his wife, may be missing her; he may want to love again, but there was nothing he *needed* from anyone. He was secure in himself. She'd never met anyone like him before. "This is all you need, isn't it?"

"*Si.*"

"Your mother was wrong, wasn't she? You're not living in the past. You loved your wife, but you don't *need* anyone."

"Maybe not 'need,' but I'd like to share my life—the good *and* the bad—with someone." He glanced at her. "A special someone."

"Good. I like to think of you, and your family, here, preserving traditions. This is your place in the world. You all belong here."

"And you? Where do you belong?"

"Not here." She shrugged. "Not anywhere really."

He turned and faced her, his expression thoughtful. "You are an enigma. You come from nowhere and tell me you're going *somewhere, anywhere*—that the *where* doesn't matter. I've never met anyone like you."

She tried to laugh, but it didn't sound convincing. "We're few and far between." She attempted to drag her eyes from his gaze but failed.

He didn't join in her laughter. Instead, he stepped closer to her, his expression serious. He brought his hand to her cheek and held it there gently, his eyes holding her gaze, intent, trying to understand. "Will you stay until the New Year?"

She opened her mouth to reply, but no word formed. Demetrio smiled and brought his other hand to her other cheek.

"Hm?"

She moved her head in his hands, trying to give a negative response but the feel of his hands on her cheek, his fingers moving in her hair under her hat made her close her eyes instead and breathe him in. She swallowed.

"Ursula?"

Then she felt his lips on hers, warm and gentle, moving over hers in a brief but sensuous kiss. She swayed toward him, and he slid his arms around her waist and pulled her under his open jacket. "Ursula? Will you stay a little longer?"

She half-shook her head and opened her mouth to speak, but his lips claimed hers once more before she could respond. And there was no thinking with his mouth upon hers, urging her to *do* and to *feel* things she couldn't remember ever having felt before. Eventually, he pulled away.

"You haven't replied."

She pressed her head against his chest. "And how am I meant to reply when you keep kissing me?"

He stepped away so he could see her clearly. "I've stopped now. Although I can't promise that if I see another negative response about to appear, I won't kiss you again."

"I can't, Demetrio."

He frowned. "Why? You said you've nothing planned until the New Year."

"Don't get me wrong, you've all been very kind. I don't know where I'd be without you. But…"

He lifted her chin with his finger. "But?"

"I don't *want* to get to know you any better."

"I don't believe that."

She slapped him playfully on the chest. "You Italians are so vain."

"It's nothing to do with vanity. More, Ms. Adamsson, to do with the way you kissed me. I don't have the wide experience of many men—I was nineteen when I married

—but I can tell when someone is enjoying a kiss or not. And you enjoyed it."

"I can't deny that."

"And yet you still maintain you have no wish to get to know me better?"

"I wish to, but I won't let myself." She pulled away. "Look around you. As you said, this is your world. It's not mine. I don't belong here, Demetrio. It's that simple. I'm not one for tradition."

"And what's so wrong with tradition?"

She shuddered. "It stifles."

"Only if it's the wrong kind of tradition. My world, here, doesn't stifle. In fact, it does the opposite. It sets me free." He narrowed his gaze which was firmly fixed on her. "What happened to you to make you say that?"

She swallowed and fixed a blank smile on her face. It was the easiest way to recount her early childhood. "After my parents split up I was sent to live with my grandmother. She lived in a mausoleum of a mansion on the outskirts of Stockholm. I had a private tutor until I was eleven and barely left the house."

"Go on."

"And then, at eleven, I was sent to boarding school in England. A strange experience for a girl whose little English she did know, was learned from storybooks and was a generation out of date."

"That must have been hard."

"It was. And I swore to myself that I'd never be trapped in one building, in one place, in one city ever again. And I haven't been."

"You haven't been tempted?"

"Yes, of course. But it never worked out. And"—she shrugged—"in hindsight, it was for the best."

He tilted his head to one side. "You're scared."

"No, I'm—"

"You can deny it all you like, but you're terrified of commitment."

"That's ridiculous."

"Is it?"

"Yes, of course. I commit to many things."

"Like what?"

"A job."

"A job for which you travel all the time."

"Friends…"

"Friends whom you fly in to see, before leaving again a few days later. Ursula, you're a beautiful woman, messed up by your childhood. And instead of addressing it, you patch it up, avoiding the real issues."

"I'm still leaving, no matter what you believe to be true of me."

"Are you?" He smiled a confident smile that confused Ursula.

"Yes."

"Ursula Adamsson, I'm going to win you round."

She shook her head. "And how are you going to do that?"

"By showing you traditions you'll like, traditions you won't want to leave behind."

"Demetrio! I'm a million miles from the traditions you and your family enjoy."

"A million miles? You can traverse a million miles, a mile at a time."

"It's too far," she said, wishing she could lie and agree with him. But she couldn't do that to him.

"If I can show you a tradition you enjoy, will you promise to extend your stay by one more day?"

"That's the craziest thing I've ever heard!"

He shrugged. "Might be crazy, but do you agree?"

She couldn't hold back the laughter that was bubbling up from deep inside, releasing the tension. "Okay. One challenge, one day. Agreed."

CHAPTER 4

It was late afternoon before they all arrived at Abbadia. Marianna had driven her mother, father and little Lorenzo, and Carolina and Tomasso had traveled with Demetrio and Ursula in the Land Rover.

Ursula helped the children out of the car and into the snowy square, serenaded by a group of carolers singing traditional songs. It was past five, but the street in front of the Commune building was bright with lights. Golden lanterns hung above the street vendor stalls, and silver lights decorated two huge Christmas trees. And it would soon be brighter still when the massive bonfire in front of the Town Hall was lit. Despite the late hour, all the shops were open, and people spilled from the cafés out onto the street, where every second person appeared to be dressed up as Santa Claus.

With the two children between Ursula and Demetrio, they made their way to Marianna's car and helped Nonna into her wheelchair. Marianna handed Lorenzo to Nonna who held him firmly under her blankets. Demetrio wheeled the chair, while Papa slipped his arm through Marianna's. For some reason Ursula couldn't fathom, both the elder children took her hands so naturally that she briefly stopped in her tracks, unable to believe what she was doing. Then Carolina tugged at her, and she was in the moment again. But certainly not her usual kind of moment.

She was wearing Marianna's coat which was as practical as Ursula's clothes were sophisticated. She hadn't had time to style her hair, and its natural wave curled around the edges of the gray woolen hat. And she'd only had time to apply the barest hint of make-up—a lick of mascara and that was it. None of her friends would have recognized her; she hardly recognized herself. But it wasn't only the lack of makeup which would have made them walk straight past, or the practical clothing. No, it was that she was holding crazy conversations with the kids, while repeatedly retrieving Lorenzo's gloves which he kept dropping over the side of the wheelchair.

After listening to a *zampognari*, a roving bagpipe player, play a traditional folk carol, Nonna allowed them to continue to the café, much to the relief of the children, who'd held their hands over their ears throughout the performance. Once Nonna and Papa were settled in the café at a table by the window, where Nonna could see everything that was going on, Ursula and Demetrio went back outside with Marianna and the children.

"I'm going to the Confectionary. Are you coming?" asked Marianna.

"No," Demetrio answered. He caught Ursula's eye and smiled. Her stomach fluttered, and she grinned back. "It's nearly six we'll go and get ready for the lighting of the torchlights and join the procession, won't we Ursula? It's an important tradition."

"If it's important," replied Ursula, "how can I say no?"

"You can't."

He took her hand and placed it on his arm. "See you later, sis."

"Be good!" said Marianna with a grin, as the children pulled her away.

Despite the cold, crisp air, Ursula was warm pressed up close to Demetrio. They arrived at the bonfire which Demetrio had helped erect, in time to watch it be blessed, and set alight. People lined up with unlit wooden torches.

"Who are these people?" Ursula asked.

"They're Torchlight Chiefs. And I'm one of them. There's one for each of the torchlights, as we call the bonfires. We'll lead the procession around all the torch-lights, setting them alight as we go."

Demetrio stepped forward, took a torch from one of the group and dipped it into the fire and the flame, flick-ering at first, suddenly caught and flared into life. Demetrio held it high, the red glow sweeping the planes of his cheeks, as he looked up at the flame.

"Ready?" he asked, his eyes dancing with an intriguing combination of fun and seduction that was enough to make a girl's heart stop.

And a girl's mind. For a moment she couldn't think what Demetrio was asking her if she was ready for. What-ever it was, she nodded in agreement. His smile widened into a grin, and they fell into step with the others, singing Christmas songs as they went from the square towards the other torchlights.

Music and song filled the air; Ursula had never been

anywhere where there was such a sense of warmth and friendliness. Old friends, curious visitors, and young and old alike greeted each other with equal enthusiasm. Ursula tried to memorize each new scene in the beautiful medieval town. She never wanted to forget any detail of that night.

When they arrived at the last torchlight, Demetrio stepped forward, climbed the ladder and carefully set the bonfire alight. Ursula turned away and looked along the route the pilgrims would have taken centuries before, now bright with burning torchlights. For the first time in her life, Ursula felt a connection with the past. She turned as Demetrio put his around her shoulders and brought her to him in a brief hug. It wasn't only the torchlights which were burning bright. And it wasn't only a connection with the past she felt. She shivered with anticipation.

Demetrio took her hand and pulled it into his coat pocket, his fingers curling around hers. "There, you'll feel warmer now."

"I have your sister's gloves on," she remonstrated. But she didn't move her hand. The strains of *Bianco Natale,* sung by school children, floated across the crisp air. Demetrio started singing, and she joined in.

"Tradition number one," he whispered against her hair. "Are you enjoying this one yet?"

"Enjoying? Yes. Convinced?" Ursula pursed her lips in a mock pout of disapproval. "I'm not sure. Perhaps I need to see more."

"You"—he squeezed her arm—"are a hard woman to please."

She looked away quickly. She'd heard those words before, on a different man's lips. She'd wanted Alessandro to herself, but he hadn't been able to commit, and they'd parted ways. They'd remained friends, but nothing more. Demetrio hadn't learned yet that what he said was true. But he would, and would he want her to stay then?

"However," he continued. "I've never been a quitter, so how about we take a detour?"

He led Ursula away from the square, up a hill toward the rear of the abbey. There, they stopped.

"What do you think of that?" he asked, indicating the view of the town spread out before them.

The ancient abbey and its buildings and walled gardens was an oasis of darkness amid the torchlights which surrounded it. Their flames licked high into the sky, creating a haze of heat and light above the town. The sound of laughter, singing, and music rose up to them in waves. And there, in that moment, with Ursula's hand in Demetrio's pocket, and the beauty of his world laid out like a jewel before them, she could no longer deny that this ceremony was an incredibly special one.

"Demetrio?" He turned to face her. "I'm convinced."

He nodded with satisfaction. "I knew you would be. So, I have that extra night out of you. Now all I have to do is find another tradition."

"For another night."

"Yes. And I *will* find one. Come on, let's go and join the others and celebrate."

Ursula wasn't clear whether they were celebrating Christmas or, from the look of satisfaction in his eyes, the fact she'd agreed to stay another night.

When they arrived back in the main square, the Christmas markets were in full swing, serving aromatic Tuscan soups and savories and cakes. The many Santa

Clauses milled around the crowds, distributing sweets and candy to the singing choirs. Children, too, were everywhere, amazed to find their families had given them some freedom on this feast day.

"Like it?" Demetrio had to shout close to her ear.

She grinned. "It's amazing."

"'Doing the torch' is a way we can all come together and celebrate, united for one night, at least."

"How many actual fires are there?"

He shrugged. "Around the county? Around fifty or so, maybe. It's said to originate with the monks who gathered in front of the Abbey on Christmas Eve. Abbadia San Alexis was only a tiny hamlet a thousand years ago. The monks and the handful of inhabitants who were subjects of the Monastery, paid homage to the Abbot and gathered around a fire and waited until midnight to celebrate Mass and the birth of the Lord."

"It's amazing. Magical."

"So, you're still okay with extending your stay by another day?"

"If you're sure I won't be a nuisance?"

He grinned. "I'm *sure* you won't be a nuisance. In fact, your presence will take the heat off me. You've heard my mother—she's always telling me I should stop living in the past."

She held her breath, tight in her throat, for a brief moment before sucking in a lungful of cold night air. "And what do you think?"

He hesitated. "I think she's probably right, but there's a difference between knowing something's right and acting on it."

She felt unreasonably disappointed. "True. It's the

difference between your head tells you and what your heart wants. It sounds like your heart is still in the past."

"I think a part of it always will be." He pushed away a strand hair from her face, his hand lingering on her cheek, and her disappointment vanished. His dark eyes searched hers, his face suddenly serious. "But that still leaves a large part willing to move forward if I find a special someone."

She swallowed and shook her head, trying to shed the spell his words had created. It was as if he'd waved a magic wand around her head, and held her captive, responsive to whatever he commanded. She shook her head again. "Ah, those special someones can be tricky to find."

He frowned. "And yet sometimes they appear out of nowhere. Like ethereal beings sent from the heavens to rescue me." He caressed her cheek. "Like you."

She could hardly concentrate with the rush of sensation the simple caress created throughout her body. But she *had* to resist. They were just words, just a touch, nothing she should take seriously. She had to break the spell. "I'm no ethereal being. And I'm pretty sure *you* rescued *me!*"

But the spell wasn't broken. Demetrio narrowed his eyes, his expression suddenly serious. "Where did you come from, Ursula?"

"I've no idea. I had no intention of coming here. It just" —she shrugged—"happened."

He brushed his thumb over her bottom lip. "That's magic for you. You can't plan for it, you can't organize it, sometimes the universe conspires to make something happen, and all we can do is accept it."

And at that moment she believed every word he said. She wanted nothing more than to be in his arms, in this place, and forget about her real life. Because there was nothing more real to her than this man, and this moment in time.

"Demetrio!"

They both jumped, and Demetrio shook his head with a smile as they looked to where his mother sat. Her shout had carried across the square, despite all the people and music.

"I feel like I'm fourteen once more and have been caught red-handed." He slid his hand down her arm until he held her hand firmly within his. His fingers curled around hers and gripped it tight. "Nonna!" he called. "We're coming."

Nonna and Marianna exchanged knowing glances as Ursula and Demetrio walked hand-in-hand towards them. Still holding Ursula's hand, Demetrio bent over and kissed his mother.

"You see?" Nonna said.

"What?" he asked, his eyes narrowing in suspicion.

His mother opened her eyes wide with a guileless expression. "The fires, of course. They're alight."

Ursula looked from Demetrio to Nonna, aware of an undercurrent of communication which, she suspected, had little to do with fires. Demetrio grinned and looked toward the center of the square, where flames licked up into the icy air. "Yes," he said. "They're well and truly lit."

The smell of the newly lit fires filled the square, mingling with the aroma of hot food. Flames shot out between the horizontally placed logs that made an outer framework of nearly eight meters to contain the fire, within which the logs were neatly stacked. It was soon white hot in the middle with an orange halo all around. It was mesmerizing.

"There's something so primitive about fire; it's hard to draw your eyes away from it," said Ursula.

"*Si*. Destructive, rejuvenating—so useful and magical if tamed, and so devastating if not controlled."

Like love, she thought. It had proved destructive in her past—so destructive she'd decided she'd never trust it again. "Like so many things, I guess."

"It'll continue to burn throughout the night. We'll return home now for dinner and then we can come back for Midnight Mass if you wish?"

Carolina and Tomasso began jumping up and down, talking ten to the dozen and demanding to go to Midnight Mass.

"No, we can't take Lorenzo, and we can't leave him with Nonna," said Marianna.

"Of course you can!" said an indignant Nonna. "You don't think I can look after a baby when I've brought you all up?"

Marianna and Demetrio exchanged glances.

"Of course Marianna doesn't think that, Nonna," said Demetrio. "But it doesn't matter as Ursula and I thought we'd skip Midnight Mass and keep you company. If you don't mind, that is?"

Nonna looked both relieved and annoyed at the same time. "Of course, if that's what you like. Orsula, you don't mind missing mass?"

"No, I'd enjoy staying home with you."

Demetrio shot her a grateful look. "Then that's settled."

As Marianna wheeled Nonna and the children away, Demetrio walked beside Ursula.

"Thank you for that. Although you're welcome to go with Marianna if you wish?"

She shook her head. "I'll come back with you. Although I'm not sure I'll be much help with the baby."

"Moral support will be fine. I'm the eldest in my family, so my mother had me carting my little sisters around at an early age." He held out his hand to her. "Come on, let's go have our second tradition of the night—"

"You can't squeeze two traditions in one night!"

"I can, and I will. Our second tradition is our Christmas Eve dinner. And I'm sure you will approve that tradition, and you will have to agree to yet another night."

"Just how many traditions do you have? Am I ever to leave?"

He shrugged and smiled. "That, Ursula, may be up to you."

She took his hand and walked across the busy square, hardly aware of all the activity, laser light displays projected on to the abbey walls, or the brass bands playing *O Holy Night*, only aware of the heat of his hand over hers, and the steady flare of warmth in his eyes. It was enough to thaw something that had been frozen for a very long time.

WITH THE TRADITIONAL Christmas Eve dinner eaten, and Marianna and the children at Midnight Mass, Nonna and Papa waited until the clock struck midnight before going to bed, leaving just the three of them still up—Demetrio, Ursula, and Lorenzo, who lay slumped over Demetrio's shoulder.

"Is he asleep yet?" whispered Demetrio. For all his experience with children, he hadn't managed to settle him in his own bed.

Ursula peered around Demetrio. Lorenzo's eyes were closed, and his breathing was regular. His reddened, plump cheek was pushed up against Demetrio's shoulder, and a pool of Lorenzo's saliva darkened Demetrio's pale t-shirt. "Yes, he's asleep."

Demetrio kissed the baby's arm which was slung under his neck and stood up. "Time to put him to bed."

Together they went to Marianna's room and carefully lay Lorenzo down in his cot. Lorenzo fidgeted once, his face twisting into a brief grimace as Demetrio and Ursula held their breath, and then he relaxed, his arms flicking up either side of his head in an attitude of surrender as he fell into a deep sleep.

"At last," said Demetrio, in a hushed voice. "I thought he'd never go off."

"Poor thing. Marianna wasn't sure if he was coming down with something or if he's teething. That trick Nonna did, pressing her finger against his gums, seemed to work well."

"Yes, although I think it's more likely to be the way I rubbed his back, and sang him a lullaby."

"It wasn't the lullaby." Ursula laughed.

"Are you saying I don't sing in tune?"

"I wouldn't be so rude! Maybe I was just thinking it was more likely to be how you rubbed his back?"

He shrugged. "It's true; I have a magic touch."

"And what's so magic about it?"

"Come here, and I'll show you."

He sat behind her and placed his hands on her shoulders and began massaging them. She groaned, relaxing instantly. "No false modesty, there. You do have a lovely touch."

He smoothed her hair away from her shoulders and moved his fingers down her backbone. She arched her back as his fingers molded over her spine, moving lower, down to the small of her back. Then with both hands, he swept up and over her shoulders, somehow sensing where the tension lay in her muscles and then massaging them until they relaxed under his fingers.

Suddenly there was a blast of cold air, and Marianna entered, with a sleepy child practically dangling from each hand. "Am I interrupting something?" She raised an eyebrow, and smiled.

"You're interrupting us recovering from your teething baby."

"Poor Lorenzo. And poor you, too. The least I can do is get you another drink. What is it you were drinking? Would you like another glass of wine? Or a hot chocolate? Would you like a slice of panettone with it?"

Ursula shook her head, and held up her half-full glass. "I'm fine, thanks. The panettone was delicious."

Demetrio moved opposite Ursula, with the remains of the fire between them. "How was Mass?"

"Crowded. But very beautiful. It always is. I wouldn't miss it for anything." Marianna looked down at Tomasso and Carolina, who was leaning heavily against her hip. "Even with these two sleepy heads. They hardly made it past the first hymn before they fell asleep."

As if to illustrate this, Tomasso slid onto the floor, fast asleep. "I'd best get them off to bed. Good night."

The fire flickered once more into life as Marianna closed the door behind them. Ursula tucked her feet under her and sipped her wine. She held it up to the now dwindling fire and swirled it around. The red flames lengthened and split in the cut-glass. Then she moved it and noticed Demetrio was looking at her, a slight frown on his face. He had a beautiful face, she decided. The dark skin and eyes, enriched and warmer than ever under the glow of the firelight. But there was a light in his eyes which had nothing to do with the firelight.

She swallowed, unnerved by his direct gaze. "Why are you frowning?"

He raised his eyebrows as if waking himself from a dream. "I'm trying to puzzle you out."

"I'm not so hard to work out."

"That's easy for you to say. You know you. I don't. Look at it from my perspective. You appear one cold and snowy night, your blonde hair brighter than the snow, like some apparition."

"And yet you stopped for me."

He sipped his wine. "You should always stop for apparitions. They may cast a spell over you."

"Good point. I'll bear that in mind."

He leaned toward her. "Trouble is, they may cast a spell over you, even if you *do* pick them up. *Especially* if you pick them up."

His face was close now, and her heart thumped heavily. He opened his lips as if to speak again, but no words came. She licked her lips. "I'm no apparition, no witch."

He shook his head. "Then, what are you?"

"I'm a woman."

"What kind of woman?"

"A lonely woman." She sat back suddenly, shocked and embarrassed by how easily the truth had slipped out.

He picked up her hand and studied it as if it held the answer to everything. His thumb swept the back of her hand, his fingers moving sensuously over her palm. She closed her eyes briefly as a wave of longing swept through her. She didn't want this need, but it was too powerful to stop now.

"I can't understand that. You have everything. Beauty, poise, intelligence, charm. Why are you sitting here in our farmhouse at Christmas?"

"You invited me."

The shift from the real to the superficial broke the tension, and he sat back and smiled. "So I did. And I'm not being an attentive host. Your glass is empty."

He rose and poured her another glass of wine. She took a deep breath. "I should be going to bed. It's been a long day."

"And have I convinced you with the age-old tradition of getting a baby to sleep, that you should stay another three nights?"

"Three?"

"Well, one was for the fire, another for Christmas Eve dinner and thirdly, little Lorenzo. All good solid traditions, you have to admit. And you also have to admit you enjoyed them all."

Ursula laughed. "Especially the crying baby."

"You were very good with Lorenzo—very patient and caring."

"I wasn't too bad, was I, considering I have absolutely no experience of babies?"

"Maybe some things are known at a cellular level. Instinctive."

She raised an eyebrow. "Sort of 'every woman knows how to be a mother' thing?"

His lips quirked. "Something like that."

"No way."

"Why are you so against having children?"

She halted the glass mid-way to her mouth, the red wine just close enough for her to smell its fruity aroma. "It's simply not for me. I don't know the first thing about children."

"You know how to comfort them when they're teething."

"No, I don't. That was just, well…"

"Instinctive?"

She smiled. "Well, maybe comforting anyone, a baby or an adult, demands the same response."

"So, are you going to give me an extra day of your company? Three traditions, three extra days?"

She shrugged. "If you're sure I won't be in the way."

"Sure, we're sure. We can return your hire car, and I'll drive you to Florence. I have some work I need to catch up on anyway."

Ursula couldn't be certain, but she sensed he'd had no plans to return to Florence so soon. "That would be nice. Very nice."

"Good. Now that's settled, tell me a bit more about yourself. Tell me what you were doing in Napoli."

"Returning from a friend's wedding." She paused as she cast her mind back to Alessandro and Emily. It was only a few days ago, but it felt much longer. The distance wasn't only in miles. Something had happened here, something which had given her a sense of perspective, an ability to look back on her relationship with Alessandro with a detachment she hadn't felt before. "My ex-boyfriend's wedding to be exact."

"Ah, I'm beginning to understand. And this ex-boyfriend, do you still love him?"

She shrugged. "I love Alessandro like a friend. I guess I'll always have a soft spot for him but we weren't right together, and his new wife is lovely and perfect for him in so many ways that I could never be."

"But you are perfect for someone else."

"I hope so. One day."

He reached out to take the glass from her hands, and their fingers tangled momentarily. She felt a flush of heat rise through her body. His unnerving gaze didn't leave hers.

"But, for now," he said quietly. "We should go to bed."

Her heart thudded against her rib cage. She wondered if Demetrio had been thinking the same as her. He smiled as if he understood her thoughts, and raised an eyebrow. "I have to rise early tomorrow, look after the farm before our visitors begin arriving. Yes, Ursula, another tradition. Christmas Day."

"I'm going to run out of time. I can see that."

He nodded slowly, a warm smile spreading across his face. "Then maybe you'll have to come here again."

Her heart leaped at the idea before her mind had any chance of controlling it. She had to draw in a deep breath before she trusted herself to reply. "Maybe."

She rose and turned off the side-lights as he turned his

attention to the fire, and together they walked up the stairs, the old wooden treads creaking underfoot. At the twist in the stairs, a round window revealed the moon, peeping between scudding clouds. She stopped and looked out. When she turned back, he was close. He stooped quickly, and his lips swept hers in a kiss that was as fleeting as it was enticing. She gasped as the breath left her body. But when she opened her eyes he was descending the stairs. He stopped at the bottom.

"I'm glad you enjoyed our traditions and that you're staying longer."

"So am I. Although I hadn't expected so many traditions in one night."

"I never said the traditions had to be spaced evenly over the days. You agreed." He smiled. "Goodnight, Ursula. Sweet dreams." It was all he said, but his dark eyes expressed so much more.

She walked to the door and began to open it.

"Ursula?" She looked down at him, hoping he was going to run up the stairs and kiss her again. "And I never said I'd play fair."

She walked inside unable to prevent a smile from spreading over her face as the door clicked closed behind her.

CHAPTER 5

The next morning Ursula descended into the kitchen a little warily. She'd slept soundly but had awoken early, her mind full of Demetrio.

She couldn't remember ever having been so drawn to a man—physically or emotionally. Her last boyfriend had been everything she'd wanted—on paper—but he'd never affected her like Demetrio. And Alessandro had always kept his distance emotionally. She'd always known exactly where she was with him, which was nowhere close to having a long-term relationship. But with Demetrio? Even after only a few days, she felt the intense pull of his personality, drawing her to him, not giving her a chance to reflect or to deny her feelings. But she *had* to deny them. They weren't real, they *couldn't* be real. She had to think of them as something she could appreciate for the next few days, and then they'd be a memory she'd always cherish. And she *would* leave. She had no choice. This wasn't her world.

She pushed open the kitchen door and was immediately assailed by the smell of delicious food cooking. Marianna was already busy at the kitchen counter, chopping and slicing vegetables. She turned around with a welcoming smile. "Sleep well?"

"Absolutely. I've never slept better, thank you. And you?"

"*Si!* All the better for having the little ones sleep in. They're still asleep. Come, help yourself to coffee and give me some sane conversation before everyone else surfaces."

Ursula poured herself a coffee and leaned against the kitchen counter. "Can I help?"

"No. Everything is in hand. Most of it is prepared. These are just a few last-minute things. We'll exchange gifts after lunch, mostly for the children." She indicated the pile of prettily wrapped gifts displayed around the pyramid-shaped *ceppo*, along with candles and other decoration. "Although we keep our special gifts until the Epiphany. Nonna prefers it that way. Twelfth Night, you know?"

Ursula nodded. She knew about Twelfth Night but had never experienced its significance first-hand. She sipped her coffee and wandered over to the *ceppo*. It was a tiered box in the shape of a tree, decorated with greenery. On the bottom shelf was the family's treasured and slightly battered *Presepio*—its Nativity scene. Decorations, fruit, nuts, and presents filled the remaining shelves. An Angel sat at the top, backlit by a pulsing electric light.

"The fruit represents gifts of the Earth," said Marianna. "The presents, gifts of man, and the *Presepio*, the gift of God."

"It's beautiful. And, sort of complete, if you know what

I mean. We had presents when I was growing up, and I remember a tree when I was very young, but now my parents and their new spouses prefer to take a vacation somewhere warm."

"Ah, that's the difference." Marianna dried her hands on a cloth and turned to Ursula. "We don't see it as a vacation, but as a celebration of family, of life." She struck a match and lit the candles which were arranged either side of each tiered shelf. Then she stood back and admired it. "There, the Tree of Light. My mother likes it lit. It reminds her of the old days before they had electricity."

A lump came to Ursula's throat, and she was unable to speak.

Marianna glanced at her. "I doubt you have such things in your house."

Ursula shook her head.

"What's your house like?" continued Marianna.

Ursula cleared her throat. "It's very Scandinavian. Wooden floors, high ceilings, plainly furnished. Quite austere really."

"Ah, like in magazines."

Ursula bit her lip. "Yes, like in magazines. Like somewhere no one with a real life would live."

Marianna touched her arm. "I didn't mean that."

Ursula lay her hand over Marianna's. "No, I know you didn't. But it's what I feel, looking at this. I can't help comparing it to my life, and my life comes up wanting."

Marianna squeezed her hand and then reached up to a shelf and retrieved a small present. "I was going to give this to you later, but I'd like you to have it now, before the screaming hoards arrived."

"Thank you!" said Ursula as she turned the small gift

in her hand. "You really shouldn't have. You and your family have already given me the gift of your company this Christmas. I feel like a cuckoo in the nest."

Marianna laughed. "A very welcome, and a very beautiful, cuckoo."

Ursula opened the small gift and laughed.

"I hope you don't mind my sense of humor," said Marianna.

Ursula inspected the wooden spoon, decorated with the direction "turn repeatedly."

"Of course not. It'll be a wonderful reminder of my time here. And, hopefully, with these instructions, I'll be able to improve my cooking skills."

Marianna hugged her. "You won't need them. But I'd like you to remember us when you're gone."

As Marianna's words lingered like the toll of a funeral bell in her mind, the door opened, and the children came rushing in, followed by a sleepy looking Demetrio. His first glance was at Ursula. He looked incredibly sexy with his eyes still full of dreams, his hair tousled and his shirt half-buttoned. And then he smiled, and she felt it deep inside her, spearing her with lust and something else, something that she knew would last well after she'd left Italy.

Christmas dinner began with a spread of antipasto, followed by pasta in broth, followed by several courses of meat, including boar *buglioni*. Chestnuts were included in everything, from the polenta through to the bread. There was panettone for dessert along with other traditional sweets, and plenty of wine with which to wash it all down. It lasted hours. It would have lasted even longer if the children hadn't been impatient for their presents, much to Nonna's disapproval.

Ursula had bought a few bits and pieces in the square on Christmas Eve, so she wasn't entirely empty-handed. And she'd supplemented these gifts with a few of her things for Marianna and the children. A small crystal bottle of perfume for Marianna, which Ursula had bought duty-free and was still unopened, a pretty mirror compact engraved with flowers for Carolina, and a small book of stories she'd picked up in Abbadia for Tomasso. After giving her presents, she glanced over and saw Nonna and Demetrio deep in private conversation as Nonna handed him something. Demetrio looked moved and, for a moment, Ursula wondered what it could be before she was caught up in the children's excitement once more.

After dinner, while young and old were either asleep or resting, Ursula cleared up the kitchen as best she could. She turned around to see Demetrio leaning against the counter watching her.

"You look as if you belong here," he said. His words gave her a rush of pleasure quite out of proportion to his light-hearted tone.

She wiped down the countertop and rinsed the cloth under the ancient tap which must have been older than Nonna. "I have a feeling that Nonna and Marianna will be searching for things for months to come."

He smiled. "That's okay. It'll keep my mother occupied. Do you want to rest, or would you like to go for a walk?"

Ursula was tired, but most definitely not *that* tired. "A walk would be lovely. I need to exercise off all that food."

"I don't think you need to exercise off anything at all."

She raised an eyebrow in query. "Really?"

He smiled and shook his head. "I think you're fine as you are."

"I'll be a few pounds heavier after that meal."

"I think you'll be just as fine with a few pounds added."

She narrowed her eyes. "And when I return to Sweden, of course, I'll lose the weight I've put on since I arrived in Italy."

He shrugged. "A few pounds lighter, and you'll be just as fine."

"I think I see a theme emerging here." She grinned.

"That you're fine?" He raised an eyebrow. "Indeed. Come on, let's go out."

THE MEDIEVAL SQUARE of Abbadia was quieter than the previous evening, but people still filled the cafés which offered food in case people were hungry after their mammoth lunches at home. But Demetrio didn't take Ursula to one of the cafés. Instead, he led her toward the abbey itself, after which the town had been named. He unlocked a side door in the high walls which surrounded the abbey, and locked it again behind them.

Immediately on passing through the high stone walls, they entered into a different world—an ancient, hushed world, far from the rush and noise of the present day. Snow lay undisturbed all around.

"Where is everyone?" asked Ursula.

"Everyone else is outside these walls. Here, we're on private land. The monks gave me a key because I've been working on a long-term plan for their estate. I've been coming back and forth over the past six months, doing test plantings, watching how things are growing, or not."

"That's very modern thinking."

"For monks?"

"Yes, I suppose I think of monks as living in the past."

"They're traditional, but then so am I. The monks don't want to turn their backs on the past, but, equally, they're not ignoring the future. Bringing the best of the past into the future, in a sustainable way, is something I'm passionate about."

He stopped walking, and Ursula took the opportunity to look about her. The impressive medieval abbey and surrounding buildings gave a solemn air to the place, making Ursula feel transitory and unimportant beside them. Some rooks, disturbed by something unseen, cawed, and flew from a copse of trees, dark against the blue sky. And all around, brilliant sunshine made the bright snow sparkle. It was a timeless scene, and Ursula knew that other people had stood where she stood, and had seen the same things she was looking at, a hundred, even a thousand years ago. There was a sense of continuity here which she'd never before experienced.

"I can see why you're passionate about this place, and about the farm. I've been all over the world and have never seen such a place as this."

Demetrio frowned. "I can't believe that. There are many such beautiful places in the world. In your own country, for example. You're simply being polite."

She shook her head. "No, no, I'm not. That's how it feels to me." She considered for a moment. "Sure, I've been to many beautiful places, but there's a different quality here."

"What?"

"I don't know. I can't put my finger on it. It's something that grips me and won't let me go."

"Then don't go."

His words hung in the air.

"I have to. I have a job, a life, apartments, family. Things to return to."

"Ah," he said. "So tell me about your life."

They began to walk toward the trees. "What would you like to know?"

"Tell me about your job. Do you enjoy it?"

She shrugged. "I used to. While I was at university studying to be a lawyer I worked on social issues in a large Stockholm law practice. I loved it. We worked with youth with problems." She shook her head. "Some of them had such terrible lives. It was a real eye-opener for me. And I felt guilty about my privileged upbringing. I decided there and then to do something about it."

"And did you?"

"For a while. For around five years I worked on youth issues. In France, as well as Sweden. But then"—she shrugged—"you know, life got in the way. I followed a man to New York and took a different job."

"How did that work out for you?"

"The man didn't work out, but the job did. I got promotions, began moving into different legal areas and I bought into a practice. It was good. But…"

"But it wasn't what you were passionate about?"

"Nowhere near. I met fascinating people and dealt

with interesting issues, but none of them gripped me. Not in the same way." She clenched her fist and held it against her heart. "None of them got me, here."

"Why don't you return to the kind of work you're passionate about?"

She shrugged. "I don't know. I haven't thought about it in a long time. I guess I got caught up in all the politics and busyness of it all. Besides, life becomes more complex as you get older, doesn't it?"

"It doesn't have to be. You can simplify it if you want to. Make one change and everything else will follow."

"You make it sound so easy."

"That's because it is. What's hard is deciding if you want to take that first step."

She paused for a moment, reflecting on what he'd said. "You're right. I have some serious soul-searching to do when I get home."

"Why wait until you're home?"

"Because I'm not sure I'm thinking very straight here." She indicated the snowy scene all around. "With all this." She bit her lip. "With you."

"Good. Because I'm not sure I *want* you to think clearly."

He stopped walking, but she didn't. She was scared she'd agree to anything if she lingered in that idyllic spot and allowed his warm words to curl around her heart. She stopped walking a few feet away and waited until he'd caught up with her.

She pressed her lips together and looked at him. "That's enough about me. Tell me about your work."

They continued along the path. "Not much to tell. I

grew up helping my father on the farm. I went away to Florence and studied to be a landscape designer and stayed on, working wherever I think I can make a difference. I've always worked with the land. I can never leave it, never be far away from it."

"So you don't travel out of Italy very much?"

"No."

"Not even the occasional trip, say, visits to Sweden?"

He shook his head. "My future is here. I'll never leave Italy. And, besides, I hate to travel. All those people, the traffic, the congestion, it drives me crazy."

"Of course." She smiled. "You prefer to travel alone, driving a tractor along empty roads, with nothing but trees all around."

He didn't smile back. "No. I prefer to drive a tractor down tree-lined, empty roads, with nothing but a beautiful woman wrapped in a blanket by my side."

"Ah, but maybe that beautiful woman feels she doesn't belong on that lonely road?"

"Then that is very sad, indeed." He reached into his pocket and withdrew a package. "And that beautiful woman might need reminding of that moment. Here, I have a gift for you. I wanted to give it to you when we were alone." He handed her a small package. "It's nothing special. Just something to remind you of us when you're gone."

She bit her lip and took the gift from him, trying to suppress the emotions that his words had brought forth. The present was wrapped in plain white paper and tied with an extravagant silver bow. She slid the package from the bow and unwrapped the paper. Inside was a snow globe with a chestnut tree at its center. She shook it and snow clouded the globe, its flakes eventually settling on the tree. She had a vision of herself doing the same thing when she was back at her apartment in Sweden, and tears sprang to her eyes.

"Ursula? Don't you like it? I'm sorry, I know it's small and inconsequential—"

"No!" She looked up, not caring that he saw her tears, only wanting to correct him. "No, not at all. It's wonderful. I love it. But you're wrong about something."

He tilted her chin up. "What's that?"

"I don't need the snow globe to remind me of here. Because I have a feeling I'm never going to forget a single minute of it."

"You're crying," he said, frowning. "Ursula?"

She swiped away her tears messily with her gloved fingers. "I'm fine," she said, betrayed by the cracked tone of her voice.

He put his hands on her cheeks and lifted her face to his. "No, you're not."

She licked her lips. "I am. Or I will be."

"Will be? When?"

"After…" She hesitated, but why wait? "After you kiss me."

He smiled and brushed his lips against hers. She felt the catch of his breath against her mouth. Then he pulled her to him and held her close. She closed her eyes as she pressed her cheek against the warmth of his coat. "Oh, Ursula."

Oh, indeed. Demetrio didn't need to say anything more to express how he felt. There was so much longing in the way he said her name—longing for something which one cannot have—and so much regret in the "oh," that she understood perfectly. She knew all about longing. She was used to that. She could still do that. She pulled away with a regretful smile. "We're two very different people, from two very different worlds."

"Are we? Are you sure about that? Are worlds really so different? Surely people have the same issues, the same problems, the same joy? Come..." He stepped away, her hand still in his. "I want to show you around the town, the parts you haven't yet seen."

They re-entered the square, and instead of going along the main street, they turned off into a narrower street. They stopped outside an old building with steps running up to a battered front door. A sign revealed it to be an advice center for the youth of Abbadia.

"There's little here for young people, without resources, to occupy themselves. So they turn to the same distractions that urban kids have. You see, Ursula, we have the same problems as everyone else, despite the beauty of the place."

The building itself also looked like it had problems. While the timber around the windows was freshly painted and brightly colored potted plants were visible inside the building, the stonework and roof tiles looked like they were in desperate need of expensive attention.

"The center doesn't look like it's thriving."

"It needs funds. It needs more good people to run it. The qualified people we need aren't interested in staying here because it doesn't help their career. They stay a year, two at the most, and then return to the cities where they can earn big money and have big careers."

"How do you know so much about it?"

"I'm on the Board of Trustees and help out at a practical level when I can. I take kids who are interested in the land out and about, and show them how they can make a difference. Some come on sufferance, but a few have been inspired to go on to study and work in conservation."

"You make a real difference to people's lives, don't you?"

"A few, maybe. Not enough. But I do what I can." He glanced at her. "You look cold. Coffee?"

She suddenly realized she felt chilled. "A coffee would be wonderful."

They walked around the corner and entered a cozy, low-beamed café that looked more like someone's kitchen than a café, and ordered coffee and cake. Demetrio found a table by the window, and they stripped off their heavy coats.

While they waited for their order, Ursula brought out her snow globe and shook it and placed it between them. "I wish I'd been able to buy you something better than the scarf." She'd given Demetrio a scarf she'd picked up in Naples which she'd bought as a last-minute present for her father.

"I don't want anything else. The scarf is perfect!" He brushed his hand down its length. "Very perfect, and very fine. And, no doubt far more expensive than my snow globe."

"Nowhere near as good." She had an idea and plucked a pen and paper from her bag. "Ah, I have it." She wrote something, and pushed it across the table to him.

"'Ursula Adamssen cordially invites Demetrio Pecora to visit her and sample Sweden's traditions.'" He grunted and pressed his lips together. "I'm afraid you're safe, there. I never leave Italy."

A shadow fell over her happiness. "I was hoping you might make an exception to claim your Christmas gift."

He took her hand. "Thank you for your gift, but my place is here. Besides, your presence has been gift enough. It's given me something I've not experienced in quite some time."

"And what's that?"

"Hope. Hope that I may have a future, after all."

She took his hand in both of hers. "Oh, Demetrio! How could you think you have no future? Your wife, Elisabetta, wouldn't want you to stop living because she did. Not if she loved you. Because that's not how love works."

"How does it work? Can you tell me? Because I'd like to know."

"I'm the last person who should be giving advice on love with my track record. But I can tell you one thing, if I loved a man and *I* died, I wouldn't rest in peace if I knew he was mourning me instead of getting on with life."

He smiled. "But that's you. I have a feeling Elisabetta would prefer me to remain single, and committed to her memory."

It was Ursula's turn to frown. "Really? But…"

"You thought Elisabetta was a saint?" He grinned. "She was a wonderful woman, and I loved her, as did my family. But she wasn't perfect. And she never tried to hide her imperfections. In fact, they were a part of what made her so…"

"Unforgettable?" suggested Ursula quietly.

He nodded. Just then the waiter brought the coffees and cakes and began talking to Demetrio, leaving Ursula with the word echoing around her mind. Even if she could surmount their differences, how could she possibly compete with an unforgettable, incredible woman who would always stay that way in the heart and mind of her husband?

CHAPTER 6

The next few days flowed one into another as family, tradition, town, and country all blended into one harmonious holiday season, which Ursula could never have imagined in her wildest dreams.

Her imagination definitely stopped short of conjuring up someone like Demetrio. She'd never met anyone like him. Their chemistry was undeniable but so was his commitment to his wife's memory and love. *And* to the land, family, and tradition of which he was an integral part. Ursula had an uneasy feeling that if any one of these three things were taken away, then he would lose something of himself. She guessed that was how he felt about his wife's death—something was missing and Ursula didn't know if anyone could fill the gap his wife had left behind.

But she pushed all her doubts to the back of her mind. She only had a few more days, and Demetrio had promised her an excursion to an unknown destination. She'd enjoy his company and not think about the future because that would come anyway, like it or not, and she had a funny feeling she wouldn't.

The road trip—thankfully not in a tractor and without a dog blanket in sight—only took fifteen minutes down the winding road, to the foot of Mount Amiata.

"Aren't you going to tell me where we're going?"

"There's a sign up ahead. It should tell you everything you need to know."

Ursula read the road sign as it flashed by. "Bagni San Filippo." She turned to Demetrio. "Baths? Here?"

"Indeed. Mount Amiata is a volcano, you know, although it's a dormant one. It has natural thermal springs flowing from deep underground. We're going just outside Bagni San Filippo to Fosso Bianco."

"Fosso Bianco? White Bones? That sounds gruesome!"

"It's the sulfur. It bleaches the landscape and the trees, giving it an eerie look. But the water reputedly has great powers. It would be a shame not to see it while you're here."

They parked at the natural spa, and the slam of the car doors sounded loud in the chill air. They looked over the fence, and Ursula gasped. Before her were spread white terraces, dotted with steaming blue pools. "Wow!"

"You can bathe in some of the pools if you like. Marianna gave me her swimsuit for you, in case you wanted to."

"But all the notices warn people not to."

He shrugged. "They're over-cautious. The council has to cover itself. But so long as you don't put your head under, and know which pool to go in, it's fine. Of course, the only problem is the lack of changing facilities."

She glanced at him shyly, as an idea formed. "We have the car."

He grinned. "I guess we do have the car, if you think that's enough?"

"Well, it'll be a bit awkward but"—she looked at the bright blue steaming pools set amidst white stone—"I can't pass this up."

They returned to the car, and Demetrio held up a towel while Ursula wriggled into Marianna's swimsuit and then pulled a thick coat over the top. She jumped out.

"Your turn!" She laughed, feeling more carefree than she'd felt in years.

He handed her the towel. "But don't worry about holding it up, no one's passing by and"—he said, with a grin—"I don't mind if you look."

In the end, she only had one quick inadvertent peek when he shifted in the seat, revealing biceps and broad shoulders that made her want to open the door and touch his bare skin. But then he turned and winked, and she lifted the towel once more into place.

He helped her over the gates, and they stood by the side of the pool. Steps were carved into the rock. "Are you sure it's safe?"

"Of course. Are you ready to take off your coat?" She shivered at the thought, looked at the snow that lay thick on the fields only meters away, but inhaled the warm, humid air of the water and nodded. "On the count of three."

"One." They began to undo their buttons.

"Two," he said, and they pushed off their trousers.

"Three." They both pulled off their coats, and Ursula cried out as the cold bit into her bare skin. Demetrio jumped in the pool, reached up and took her hand, and she was soon submerged up to her neck in the hot pool.

"Oh, my…" She sighed and closed her eyes against the bright sunshine. "This is wonderful." The stone was smooth where she sat, and she stretched her legs out in the milky blue pool and splashed her toes, sending ripples across the surface. "Your country is so strange! Frozen waterfalls on one side, and hot pools, the other."

"What can I say? We like variety."

"So do I."

He waded over and sat beside her. "Glad you came?"

She closed her eyes. "Sure am."

"So am I. I thought the hotel spa would suit you better, but I was wrong."

She opened her eyes, suddenly thoughtful. "Yes, I can see why you'd think I'm a hotel-type of girl. I would have agreed a week ago. And it's only now I can see what I've been missing."

Demetrio tilted his head towards her so she couldn't help but look into his eyes. "And what can you see now?"

She smiled slowly. "There's only thing, one person, who's filling my vision."

"Good," he said, a smile playing on his lips.

She laughed and poked her finger at his chest. "You, Demetrio Pecora, are a stereotypical macho Italian male."

He raised an eyebrow and grabbed her finger. "I should hope so. But if you wish to elaborate I won't stop you."

"You wish to be the center of a woman's attention."

"*Si!* Of course. What man wouldn't?"

She sighed. He was incorrigible. "And, for another thing, you're completely absorbed in your family."

"And why wouldn't I be, with a wonderful family such as mine? What would be the point of anything, otherwise?"

She refused to accept the logic of his argument. "And for another—"

But before she could speak he took her finger and grazed his lips along it, before lifting it and kissing her palm with a sensuousness which wiped any thoughts from her mind. Except for one.

"Demetrio, I…"

"*Cara*, you're right. I'm a full-blooded Italian male, but there's one thing you missed out."

"And that is?"

"I want to know your body better; I want to pleasure you."

She grew instantly hotter "Oh." She exhaled, weak at the thought of making love to Demetrio in a public spa. It should have sent her running. Instead, it sent her body humming with lust, and her mind racing.

He kissed her, and she opened her mouth beneath his probing tongue, as a moan formed in her throat. His hand swept around the small of her naked back, and he pulled her toward him until she found herself seated on his lap.

As the kiss deepened, she lost any shred of resistance as his hands explored her back, her waist and the curves of her bottom. She felt she'd have done anything he asked, there and then. And, when his hands lingered on her bottom but moved no further to other places where she was longing to be touched, she wriggled on him, wanting him to lose his control, wanting his breathing to become as ragged as hers. But he pulled back and, instead a smile hovered on his lips. He pushed her wet hair away from her face. "You are crazy wonderful. So sweet. So many things."

"And *you* are so controlled."

"Just as well one of us is." He grinned as he lifted her off him. "Don't misunderstand me, *cara*, I want to make love to you. But not in the open—despite the fact we are alone—and not in the car. And not in a hotel room. That would not be making love, that would be taking you. And I never want to do that. Maybe pleasure you a little, but making love? That must wait until everything is perfect."

"What if I want to be taken?"

He wasn't smiling now. "You may think you do, but it won't give you the memories I wish to give you. For that, we must go to Florence. There I can make love to you as I wish to."

"And how do you wish to?"

"Slowly, thoroughly, repeatedly," he said with a grin.

She sighed and sunk lower into the pool, hoping its heat would be excuse enough for her flushed skin. "Oh my! So..."

"Yes?" He caressed her neck.

"I was just wondering whether we should cut short our stay in Abbadia. Maybe go straight to Florence?"

"Not yet, Ursula. You promised a few more days, yes?"

"But that was before you'd described what you plan to do with me there."

He shifted closer to her and played with her hair. "Maybe if I elaborate on those plans a little, describe in detail what will happen, and maybe give you a little pleasure now, then you'll be content to stay."

She shrugged. "Maybe. It's worth a try."

He trailed his finger down her cheek, her neck,

pausing on his downward movement, to briefly caress the dip at the base of her throat. "Here goes…"

Ursula's breath hitched, and her eyes fluttered closed as Demetrio's words caressed her every bit as effectively as his hands.

~

LATER THAT NIGHT, after a long, protracted and delicious dinner, Nonna reiterated her invitation for Ursula to continue her stay until Twelfth Night.

"You should stay, Ursula. Twelfth Night is the proper festival."

"You've been more than kind offering me your hospitality over the past week. But I can't stay any longer. I have to return to work."

"And your family. No doubt they are anxious for your return."

Ursula's smile faded, and she shrugged. "I guess." She nodded too vigorously to convince Demetrio whose brow was raised in query. "Although they're all pretty busy." But her reply appeared to satisfy the rest of his family who turned to watch Carolina sing a Christmas carol.

Demetrio pushed away his plate. "Ursula, if your family are busy elsewhere, what's to stop you from staying until Twelfth Night, as my mother suggests?"

"I can't keep extending my stay, Demetrio. I need to return to my life at some point."

"Then why don't you make that point *after* Twelfth Night? I'd like you to stay," he added quietly.

She escaped answering by the arrival of Marianna and a plate of sweets. As she engaged in conversation with

Marianna, wanting to keep her with them as long as possible so she could avoid answering Demetrio, Demetrio's father called him away. Only then, once the pressure was off, could she relax, and consider Demetrio's request. They'd gotten so close that afternoon, physically and emotionally, but still there was a barrier between them which she couldn't imagine being overcome.

Was she reading too much into everything, imagining this whole thing between them? It wouldn't be the first time that a romance which existed in her mind didn't mirror reality. What if he was just being polite? She didn't think she could stand it if he was. Because she was falling for him as surely as if she were tumbling headlong down a steep hill with nothing to stop her fall.

But what had he really said? Nothing more than his mother had said. But then there were the kisses… and more. But, he was a man, and in her experience men's physical drive had no connection to their emotions. No, she had to stop it now because if she stayed, she'd only fall harder for him, delay the pain she'd feel when they parted. Why postpone the inevitable?

Demetrio returned and sat down. "So, have you thought about it? Will you stay?"

She smiled a bright and breezy smile and stood up. "It's so kind of you to invite me. But I have to go."

His eyes narrowed, and he looked away quickly. She rose and took her plate to the kitchen sink and began talking to Marianna. Ursula glanced at him and he caught her gaze. She looked away again quickly.

"Then, Ursula"—she turned to find him standing staring at her with a determined look on his face—"we should return to Florence tomorrow."

"But I can use the hire car—it's still in the garage."

"No, I'll take you. The road is treacherous at this time of year, and I'll return in a few days. You're welcome to stay at my apartment the night before your flight leaves, or a hotel. Whichever you prefer."

She nodded hesitantly. "Thank you."

"No problem," he said in the coolest tone she'd heard him use since she'd arrived. She returned to the kitchen sink, only glancing around as he grabbed his jacket and headed out the door.

"Demetrio!" called Nonna, after him. "Where's that boy gone to now?"

Marianna glanced at Ursula who couldn't meet her eye. What had she done? But she knew. She'd hurt someone who'd offered her nothing but kindness.

CHAPTER 7

It had been hard to say goodbye to everyone, knowing she would never see them again. Because how could she? They wouldn't be visiting Sweden anytime soon, and her? How could she return to these wonderful people, and not torture herself with wanting what she couldn't have?

And if leaving Abbadia had been difficult, the journey to Florence with Demetrio was even more difficult. After five minutes of silence, Ursula cracked.

"I'm sorry, Demetrio. But I couldn't stay. I just couldn't."

He didn't even turn to look at her. "I understand," he said coolly, before checking his rear vision mirror and overtaking a truck.

"And what exactly do you think you understand?" She was beginning to feel annoyed. Why should he be irritated that she didn't do as he wanted? Did he think she was ungrateful, or was he angry he hadn't gotten his way?

"That you're scared, of course. Scared to make a decision that could change your life." He shrugged. "It's a shame. I'd hoped you would."

Her anger deflated. That wasn't how the script had run in her head. "How can I make a decision that would change my life based on a few days with strangers?"

That made him look at her, but the coolness in his glance made her wish he hadn't. "Strangers? Is that what we are? Even now?"

"No, of course not. But… still, I can't turn my whole life around, based on a few days. Even if they *were* a fantastic few days, it would be rash."

"Risky even," he added.

"Risky, rash."

"Plain foolish." His face betrayed no emotion.

"Exactly."

"Okay, I get it, Ursula. How about we simply enjoy our last night together? We can go out and meet my friends, and I can meet the friend you were telling me about and have some fun? No strings, no demands. Just nice, simple fun? Yes?"

She sighed. "Yes. Nice. Simple. Fun. I like the sound of that."

"WELL, THIS IS IT."

Demetrio watched as Ursula stepped into his apartment. "Apartment" was a grand name for something so small.

He was suddenly aware of how homely, how ramshackle his surroundings were. Especially when compared to Ursula. She walked into the room like a white swan gazing upon a muddy duck pond, as if she knew it were *possible* for someone to live there, but she couldn't imagine how.

Irritated by the comparison that had instantly sprung to mind, Demetrio went to the kitchen and plucked some cups and glasses from the wooden shelves he'd built.

He followed her gaze around the dark painted walls—the books, lamps and things of sentimental value to him—to the battered brown leather settees with mismatched cushions, some of which his sisters had made at school.

"It's… lovely," Ursula said. "So…"

"Homely?"

She turned to face him, alert to his ironic tone. "It's homely in the sense that it's a home, but not in the sense it's plain. No, I was going to say it's so… *you*."

It didn't reassure him. "Right. Well, would you like tea, coffee or a glass of wine?" He tried to remove the spike from his voice, but knew it was still there by her frown.

"Wine would be lovely." She sat on the buttoned leather sedan, and ran her hand over the table he'd made from one of his own trees, which had been struck by lightning. "You made this?"

"Yep. I guess it's pretty obvious. Couldn't buy something like that, if you tried. And who'd try?" He winced as he turned his back to her. What the hell was he doing? Making light of something that was important to him. He'd poured his heart and soul into that table, deciding not to deepen the colors with oils, but to lighten them to better reveal the grain. It was like looking a tree made silver by moonlight.

"Just about anyone," Ursula said. "And the way you've finished it looks amazing with the retro black leather."

"Retro?" He grunted. "I suppose it is. I inherited it from a great aunt of mine—my grandfather's sister, who was an artist." He indicated a small painting on the wall. "She painted that."

Ursula rose to look at the painting. "It's Abbadia San Alexis, isn't it?"

The way she said the name of his hometown was beautiful. He walked up behind her, ostensibly to better see the painting, but instead studied the fall of her hair. He'd never seen hair that color before, so pure and vivid. He wanted to touch it. Instead, he thrust his hands into his pockets. "*Si*. It's the waterfall in summer." He pointed to a figure in the foreground. "That's my father when he was young, with the rest of his siblings. I did the same thing when I was that age. And no doubt my grandfather did, too."

"I can't imagine being tied to one place like you are to Abbadia."

"A tie?" The reverie broken, he returned to the kitchen. "A tie," he repeated. "Like a shackle, a ball and chain, an unwilling connection."

"I didn't mean that." She turned to him. "A connection is a connection. And your family has it with this land. Why are you trying to twist my words?"

He sighed, set down two glasses and smiled ruefully. "Maybe it's my turn to be defensive. It wasn't just the settee I inherited from my great aunt, but this apartment, too. I've had it since I was eighteen, built those shelves, brought things into it. Old things, of course."

"It's beautiful."

"I'm sure you don't really think that." He opened a bottle of wine and poured two glasses. When he turned back, she was standing with her arms crossed, mouth stern.

"And why would I say it, if I didn't think it?"

He looked around the apartment, trying to see it through her eyes. The apartment reflected him and all that he held dear in his life. But it was also an accumulation of other people, other times. He hadn't thought about it before but, as he looked around, he realized he hadn't brought anything new into this apartment until now. Until Ursula.

Up till now, he'd been living in some frozen state, stuck in the past, and he hadn't even known it. He'd accused Ursula of being unavailable emotionally when, all along, he had been, too. It had taken him to look at his apartment through Ursula's eyes to understand that, while he may have been happy enough before he met her, his life had been a shadow of what it could have been—a shadow of what it could be, with her. He loved her, and he couldn't bear to let this new-found radiance shine its light away from him.

He placed the glasses on the table, and they sat on opposite sides. A silence descended during which they exchanged awkward glances as they sipped their drinks.

"So… your last evening." He smiled briefly. "I've run out of traditions to keep you."

She looked away, and he couldn't tell what she was thinking. And he didn't want to know either, in case he didn't like it.

He jumped up and strode over to the window. "Looks like it's stopped snowing. It's forecast to thaw tomorrow. You shouldn't have any problems flying out of Florence."

"I *have* to go, Demetrio. I have to return to my life. It's not like you need me here. You have your family, your world. Your life is here. Mine isn't."

Surely she had to see that he wanted her to stay? He'd practically been begging her not to leave every day since she'd arrived. He'd managed to get a few extra days out of her, but he couldn't go on asking her to stay. It had to come from her.

"Demetrio?" Her soft voice was right behind him. He turned around and the sight of her blonde hair, even brighter in the reflected light of the snowy world outside, made the breath catch in his throat. The message in her blue, almond-shaped eyes was clear—she wanted something. But what it was he didn't know, but he was going to find out.

"Tell me, Ursula"—he raised his hand and stroked her silky hair—"what is it you want?"

"Can't you guess?"

He shook his head, not daring to hope.

"I want *you*, of course."

He groaned and reached out and brought her face to his, holding her steady, not wanting her to escape, not yet. But he needn't have worried. Her only movements were toward him, not away from him.

It was she who lifted her face to his and kissed him. But not tentatively, there was no diffidence in the kiss. She took control, pressing her lips to his with an urgency which surprised him. She always seemed so in control, so calm, that he was shocked to feel the depth of need that lay beneath the surface. He opened his mouth, and her tongue slid against his.

She gasped against his open mouth as she pressed closer. She moved against him, exploring his body with her own, just as her tongue and mouth explored his. Her hands spread over his back and lower, over his behind, pressing him even harder against her.

Their movements quickened, as desire overtook them. She slipped her fingers under his shirt, caressing the bare skin beneath, just as his hands ranged over her body, taking in the curves of her shoulders, the indentation of her lower back and then down to her behind, lifting her against him.

Still kissing, she curled her legs around him, and he carried her to the bedroom. They fell onto the bed, side by side. They lay for several minutes, the kiss broken, gazing into each other's eyes. He pushed away the hair that had fallen across her face and stroked her cheek with a shaking hand.

She touched his hand. "You're shaking. Why?"

"I want you so much, I've thought about you so much, but I hardly dared hope that you might… "

"Demetrio," she whispered, licking her lips, "I've just jumped on you, kissed you, pressed my body against yours." She leaned in and slid her tongue across his lower lip, then pulled back to see its effect. "What else can I do to prove I want you?"

He grinned. "Take off your clothes?"

She raised her eyebrows but didn't grin back. She rose and pulled off her jersey. Then she began to undo the buttons of her shirt. His eyes moved to each button as she undid it, revealing a black t-shirt. She tossed the white shirt across the room with a stripper-like flourish and turned back to him, hands on hips. "You want more?"

"So long as it doesn't take too much time." He swallowed. "Otherwise I'll be tempted to help you along."

She didn't need telling twice. She pulled her t-shirt over her head and quickly shed her jeans, leaving her standing in only her lacy underwear.

She looked endearingly unsure and awkward, which she compensated for by a quick lift of the head.

"Come here," he said.

And she came, and his lips met hers with a swift, reassuring kiss. As his mouth kept hers busy, his hands slid lower, intent on exploring her intimately. She gasped at his touch.

"*Now* do you know understand how much I want you?" she whispered into his hair, as her body quivered under his caress.

He nuzzled her neck. "I'm beginning to get the message. But if you'd like to show me further, go ahead."

She grinned and shook her head as she rose to kneeling and pushed him back onto the bed. "You're bringing out the worst in me, Demetrio Pecora."

"Good. Go ahead and show me your worst, and then I'll show you mine."

He could feel the bubble of her laughter rise and enter him as she kissed him and he knew that seeing Ursula at her worst would be the best thing that had happened to him in years.

MUCH LATER, Ursula awoke to see Demetrio silhouetted against the un-curtained window, the lights of Florence spread jewel-like before him.

She rose, rested her hand on his shoulder, and leaned her naked body against his. He turned, dropped a kiss on her cheek, and slipped his arm around her hips, bringing her tight against him.

"Did I wake you?" he asked.

She shrugged. "Maybe. I don't know. Maybe your absence awoke me. What are you looking at?"

"Nothing in particular. Just thinking."

"About what?"

"You." He smiled at her. "Me."

"Two big subjects."

He turned to her, the cool light limning one side of his body; the other side, dark. In that strange light, she realized how little she knew him—he was half-stranger, half-lover. She felt a tremor of fear flicker through her, and she drew away.

He frowned. "What's the matter? Cold?" She shook her head but, despite her denial, he reached for the throw on the leather chair and brought it around her. "Come on, let's get back to bed."

They lay in each other's arms in silence for a while, both gazing out into the slowly brightening sky, and listening to the pealing of the church bells which signaled that morning was edging closer.

"Would you believe me if I said making love in Florence on the last Monday of the year is an Italian tradition?"

She half-laughed and shook her head. "No."

"So no more days to bargain with, then."

She looked away with studied casualness. "No, I have a busy schedule. I have a lot on."

"Of course," he replied, too quickly.

"I have to leave today." She twisted in his arms to face him. "It's time, Demetrio. This can't go on forever."

The expression in his eyes caught at her heart, as his gaze raked her features—at her hair that he pushed away, at her lips, at her throat, leaving her eyes until last. "Can't it?"

She swallowed. His words echoed in her mind and hammered against the walls of her firm intentions. "I have a life. I have a job. I have friends, a family. I can't give everything away, surrender my whole life for a dream."

"A dream?" He shook his head in confusion. "A dream?" he repeated. "Is that how you see this? Something not real, something ephemeral?"

"Demetrio! How else can I see it? You emerged from the snow to rescue me, you took me to the fire and warmed me, showed me your life. I *love* your life, but it's not for me. I'm not of your world. We both have to face the fact that I'm a misfit. There's nothing for me here." She waited, hoping against hope that he would say words that would sway her, make her stay. Because without those words she couldn't risk everything. Not again.

But they didn't come.

CHAPTER 8

Demetrio awoke and immediately reached for the warmth of Ursula's body. But it wasn't there. He propped himself up, and looked down to where she'd lain. There was only an empty space.

He rubbed his eyes, and glanced out the window. The icy gleam of early morning framed the heavy drapes. He rose, pulled on his jeans and pushed aside the curtains. Before him, Florence lay white under a soft gray sky. Snow was falling. The weather forecasters had got it wrong—there was no thaw.

He heard the sound of the shower being turned on, quickly followed by a radio—some pop song which didn't sound like anything she'd listen to. He waited for her to change stations, or to turn it off. She did neither. And he knew then that she was hiding behind the noise. Something had happened. Something was up. He could sense it.

He pulled on a jersey and turned back to the window, pushing them open and letting in the dull peal of a church bell. He stepped out onto the small balcony, needing the icy air inside his lungs to cauterize the pain that had sprung up at the realization that Ursula was preparing to leave him. Snow had settled on the domes and rooftops of Florence. A motorino broke the silence as it roared up the road, leaving a dark track in its wake. He took another frigid lungful of air and returned inside, closing the doors tight.

Shaking off the stray flakes of snow from his hair, he went into the kitchen and switched on the coffee machine before turning on the oven to warm some croissants. He heard the bathroom door open, and Ursula moving around the bedroom. He wanted to go to her. He gripped the edge of the counter and leaned into it, willing himself not to go and take her in his arms. It wouldn't do any good, forcing her to him, forcing her to stay. It would do the opposite. It would give her a reason to leave. As it stood, she had no reason to leave, and he refused to give her one.

"Demetrio! That smells wonderful," said Ursula as she entered the kitchen. She hesitated but, instead of coming over to him, she slid onto the seat on the far side of the table. She looked up at him and smiled. But that shy smile was a pale imitation of her former smile—it was like the sun, hidden by clouds, dimmed by the shadows of her doubts in her now guarded eyes.

He wanted nothing more than to banish those shadows, to connect with her again. He walked over and nuzzled her neck. "And so do you," he murmured. She responded immediately, and he felt a very male sense of satisfaction. He wanted to blast that shadow out of her head and heart. The whimper that came from her throat made him devote both hands to her shoulders, easing the tension away.

She turned her head, and he kissed her. When they finally drew apart, the smell of burning filled the room.

He cursed and raced over to the oven and pulled out the tray, dropping it, and the burned pastries, onto a chopping board as the heat seared through the tea towel. He cursed again as he ran his hand under cold water.

She came up behind him, put her arms around his waist and lay her cheek against his back. "It doesn't matter. I happen to like my pastries well done, with a dry-ish middle."

She picked one up, blew on it and took a bite. But there was no way she could pull anything other than a grimace.

"Tell you what, you go shower and I'll fix us some breakfast," she said.

"Okay." He put his arms around her and kissed her. "On one condition."

"And that is?"

"I get to show you one more tradition. A tradition that will keep you here a little longer." As soon as the words escaped him, he wished he could have unsaid them. It was in her swift side-ways glance. He sighed. He wondered if he'd find the right time to give her his mother's gift. He swept the hair from her face, and kissed her again. "But only if you wish it. Think about it while I shower."

DEMETRIO STEPPED out of the bathroom, rubbing his hair with a towel. He tossed the towel into the bathroom and walked towards Ursula who had her back to him. He lifted her hair and kissed her neck.

"Um, you smell so good. What is it?" He slipped his arms around her waist and brought her close against his body which was already hard for her.

"Perfume." She turned with a smile on her lips. "But we have no time for this. We're meeting Ruby, remember."

"Ah, Ruby." His mood suddenly soured. He didn't know Ruby and, from the things Ursula had told him about her, he felt he, and his world, didn't stand a chance when compared to the glamorous society in which Ruby moved.

"Yes, Ruby. I'm sure you'll like her."

"I'm sure I will," he said, doubting every word.

"She's great company, as well as a kind and caring person."

"Well, in that case, I look forward to meeting her." He tried to sound convincing but, judging from Ursula's expression, he doubted he'd succeeded.

THEY WALKED down the snowy streets of Florence to the café where they were to meet Ruby. The mellifluous sound of a saxophone escaped the old building. Once they were inside the unadorned space, the noise levels were high with music and the sound of wall-to-wall people. Demetrio tugged at his shirt collar, as claustrophobia threatened to overwhelm him.

"I thought we were meeting just Ruby."

"We never meet 'just Ruby'! She doesn't like to be alone."

Demetrio frowned. "That's odd."

"Not *so* odd, not once you know Ruby. She hasn't had an easy life." She waved at someone. "There she is!"

He looked at the tall, glamorous blonde with the outrageously stylish clothes, and couldn't imagine what kind of trouble the woman who was waving at them could possibly have.

They walked up to the group, and Demetrio's heart sank further as everyone turned to greet Ursula and looked at him askance. He was acutely aware that his casual clothes made him stand out amongst this glittering crowd.

"Ursula, darling!" A man introduced to him as Tony, greeted her. He drew her to him, and embraced her so closely that Demetrio almost growled. He stepped forward beside Ursula, and she turned to him with a hesitant smile.

"Tony, this is Demetrio."

The man looked at him, openly puzzled. "Demetrio? How nice," was all he said. It was clear that "nice," meant "how quaint."

"Tony's in fashion," Ursula said to Demetrio by way of explanation.

"Ah," said Demetrio, thinking that made sense. "I'm not interested in fashion, myself."

"Yes," Tony said. "So I see."

"Demetrio's also in design," said Ursula, too brightly.

"Oh yes?" said Tony. His lips curved into an ironic smile, but his eyes held an arrogance which Demetrio had a hard job not punching off his face. "Designing what exactly?"

"Ursula's over-selling me," said Demetrio glancing at her. "I work on the land."

"Oh! You're a farmer."

"That's right."

Ursula frowned at Demetrio. "You're a landscape designer."

He shrugged. "If you say so."

Tony looked from one to the other with a bemused smile. "Sounds like you don't agree."

Ursula's smile froze a little as she turned back to her friend. "Demetrio is a man of many talents. Farmer, landscape designer."

"Sounds as if he's confused to me." Tony raised an eyebrow.

Demetrio put his arm around Ursula. "I'm not confused. I know exactly what I do, and exactly what I want. It seems to me I'm probably one of the few who does."

He caught Ursula's gaze but didn't take his arm away.

Tony gave Ursula a sympathetic smile. He touched her hand. "Catch up with you later, Urs, when you're not so tied up."

Demetrio glared at the man's back as he walked away. Ursula turned in his arms. "What are you doing, Demetrio?"

He stuffed his hands in his pockets. "What do you mean? I'm talking to people, socializing."

"Well, if that's socializing, I'd hate to see you when you're angry about something."

Demetrio sighed and raked his fingers through his hair. "I'm sorry, Ursula, but that guy pushed the wrong buttons."

"Tony? What did he say that was so out of place?"

"It wasn't *what* he said. It was the *way* he said it, the way he looked at me—like I was from another planet." He paused. "Like I didn't fit in."

"That's just Tony. There's no need to take anything he says personally."

"You see, right there, is where we differ. I assume that when people talk, they mean what they say. What's the point in talking otherwise?"

She smiled. "These people aren't like you, Demetrio. They just talk about anything." She glanced around. "Mostly each other, to be truthful."

"I don't like that, Ursula. I don't belong here. Not with them." He studied her, waiting to see how she'd react.

The smile fell from her face, and she bit her lip and looked around. She sighed and then looked back at him. "What you're saying is that you don't belong with me, is that it?"

"No. I'm saying my world is different to theirs. I'm saying that you have to choose between them. Because I can't do this one."

"They're not like you imagine. Take Ruby; she's a wonderful woman."

"She may be. I don't know her. From what I've seen she fits well into this world. So do you. *I* don't. Now, I'm leaving and if you want to come, you can. But if you'd rather come later, then that's fine too."

"I'll just find Ruby to see goodbye and then we'll leave. Okay?"

"Sure. I'll meet you at the door."

He retrieved their coats from the lobby and watched Ursula move across the room, her blonde hair like sunshine, her fine clothes blending easily with the rest of them. What the hell was he thinking? She was way out of his league. She might as well be from Mars. She was a socialite with all the right connections. She knew what to wear, and how to talk to these people. And he? He was a farmer. He'd got that bit right, at least.

He pushed himself off the wall when she approached. "Ready?"

She nodded uncertainly. "Sure."

They walked along the snowy street in silence. They stopped at the bridge, and Ursula walked up to the railing and looked down at the icy river, its current swirling around small frozen pockets on its surface. "I've never seen the river frozen. I've only ever been here in the summer before."

Outside, Ursula had shed the sheen and glamor of the club, and he saw her as she truly was once more. He sighed with relief—the tension suddenly eased.

"I'm sorry, Ursula."

Her cheeks were flushed with the cold, her eyes bright. "What for?"

"For being such an idiot in there, with your friends."

She grinned. "You know, they're not my close friends. Apart from Ruby, that is. And I can understand why you didn't hit it off with her straight away. She's complicated."

"I should have tried harder. But you know?"

He slid his hands up the lapels of her coat, and she wriggled closer to him.

"What?"

"I was scared. You seemed different in there, with them."

She frowned. "I didn't mean to be. Was I?"

"A little, maybe. But I should have handled it better."

She cocked her head to one side. "Yes, you should."

He narrowed his gaze. "But the way that guy looked at you, I couldn't handle it. No red-blooded Italian man could."

"He didn't mean anything by it."

"He wanted you. And I didn't want him to want you."

She narrowed her eyes. "It doesn't matter what he wanted. I didn't want him, and that's an end to the matter. When I go out with someone, I don't expect to be tied to a leash. I expect to have my independence. Wasn't your wife independent? Didn't she lead her own life?"

"She was my wife and a part of my family. She led her own life within those ties."

She bit her lip, and stepped away. "There are those ties again." She huffed. "It's not a word I use much. I think of ties as holding someone in place, preventing them from moving."

"And *I* think of ties as connecting people to each other, to a place, to a home."

The silence collected around them, like the snow. Cars and motorini passed less frequently now that the snow was thickening and, in this quiet cul-de-sac, with the river one side and a grand old building the other, they were quite alone, surrounded by the icy silence.

It was Ursula who broke the spell first. She turned abruptly and took a couple of steps away from him. "Looks like we have quite different ideas about such things."

He fisted his hands in his pockets. "I guess it's time to go."

They walked side-by-side to the apartment, no longer

holding hands. He held the door open for her, and she ran up the steps. He followed, taking them two at a time.

"Coffee?" he asked as they entered the apartment.

"Sure, that would be great." She pulled off her hat, and her tumble of white-blonde hair made his heart ache because he no longer felt able to touch it. "I'll just… just go and get out of these wet clothes."

He made the coffee, but she hadn't emerged. So he pushed the door open and took the coffees to her. She was kneeling by the bed, smoothing the last item into a suitcase before she clicked the case closed. She turned around, and saw him.

"I'm sorry, it's just…"

"Just that you thought you'd take the opportunity to pack your bags." He placed the coffee on the bedside cabinet, pushed his fingers through his wet hair and walked away from her. "Sure. Good idea." He couldn't prevent the bitterness he felt from spilling into his voice.

"You're angry. I understand—"

"You understand, what exactly? Tell me, because I don't think *I* understand. I'd like you to stay. I can't believe you don't feel anything, not after what's happened between us."

"Honestly? I don't know what I feel. I don't know if I *can* feel."

"There's only one way to find out. Stay and try."

For one long moment, Ursula didn't move. Their tangled gaze was unwavering. Then she glanced away, and he knew he'd lost her.

"I have to go. You know that. But I'll be back… no doubt."

"No doubt," Demetrio replied too quickly.

"Demetrio, it's not that simple."

"Isn't it?"

"No, of course not. I have work, I have a life, friends, family, all of which is elsewhere."

"You could have all of those things here if you wanted to."

Ursula shook her head. "A life? With you wanting to tie me down? Friends, when we're such different people and have such different tastes in people?"

He took her hands in his. "Ursula, none of that means anything. Can't you tell I'm crazy about you?"

"But… but we hardly know each other."

"We've known each other a week. How long is the correct amount of time to know what I feel for you is true? One month? One year? Five?" He shook his head. "No, Ursula, it doesn't work like that. I knew within five minutes of meeting you that I wanted to be with you."

"Five minutes?"

He would have smiled at her astounded face if it hadn't made him feel so sad. "You're right. That's a lie. It was more like three minutes. When you *know*, you *know*. You either love someone, or you don't. I love you but, it seems, you don't love me."

"Demetrio… I…"

"It's okay." He kissed her hands swiftly and dropped them. "You don't have to say anything further. I understand." He opened the fridge, buying time as he pretended to look for some food, closing his eyes against the chill, praying it would calm him, stop his heart from pounding as if it would break. He exhaled roughly, plucked a pot of yogurt from the fridge and put it on the table. He took a further few seconds and deep breaths before turning back to Ursula and passing her the plate. "Coffee and cake?"

She took it with a hesitant smile. "Thank you." But she didn't move, just stood there uncertainly. It made him want to grab her, show her exactly how certain she *should* feel. "Look, Demetrio. I'm so sorry, but I'm different to you and your family. You're all so loving, and I'm, well… I'm not." She shrugged.

Frowning, he shook his head, perplexed. "What the hell are you talking about?" He placed a coffee pot on the table, too firmly, spilling a little on the table's pale surface, and turned to face her, allowing his frustration to show. "Not loving? You have a generous, kind and loving heart. I've seen you with my family, *and* with me. Who are you trying to kid by saying that?"

She shrugged uncertainly. The long pause that followed was punctuated by the metallic chime of a church bell that traveled eerily across the frozen city. "Me." She drew in a deep breath and looked up, and he could see the fear in her eyes. "It could easily be me I'm trying to kid."

"And why would you want to kid yourself?"

"I don't know. Perhaps, because it's easier. Perhaps, because it's what I always do. Or, perhaps, because I've spent so long distancing myself from my emotions, I don't know if I can feel… can *love*," she added tentatively.

He gripped her by the shoulders. "Look, Ursula, I don't know what happened in your past to make you so afraid to love. I don't know whether it's only that, or whether you simply don't love me. And I'll never know until *you* do."

They stared at each other in an impasse that no words

could break. It was the tear that trickled down her face that undid him. The anger that had been his friend, that had valiantly been trying to numb the hurt, disappeared in a heartbeat. He pulled her to him, wrapping his arms around her, holding her like he'd been aching to hold her since she awoken and put the distance between them. He stroked her hair. "Ursula." He kissed her head as he felt her shake in his arms. "I'm sorry. I don't want to make it hard for you, I don't want to upset you."

She tried to speak, but only a sob emerged.

"Ursula, you're scared. I understand. But I can't help you. You'll have to work this out on your own; you have to decide on your own what you feel for me."

She shook her head and stepped away, rubbing her sleeve over her eyes. "I've never cried as much in my whole life, as I have since I met you." She paced up to the window and looked out at the sun that was already dipping behind the buildings.

"That doesn't sound like a good thing."

"Good, bad, I don't know. But it's a *thing* all right."

"Don't worry about it. Crying is fine with me."

"You see? You want some weak woman—a woman who cooks, who has babies, who cleans, and who cries. That's not me."

"I don't want '*a* woman' who does any specific list of things, at all. And I don't want a *weak* woman; there's nothing weak about crying."

She twisted around. "Nothing weak about crying? You try telling my grandmother that! She kept a cane specially to punish signs of weakness." Ursula sighed heavily, and looked up at the ceiling. "She had to use it a lot in the early days when I didn't want to go to boarding school.

And then, not so much. After a while boarding school became preferable. Being absent from my home, from my things, from my family, was a much better proposition."

"Ursula, what the hell did they do to you?"

"They did what they thought they had to do to toughen me up, to make me fit into the real world. I learned early, and I don't know if I can unlearn. I don't know if I can be the woman you want me to be."

He shook his head. "Don't you understand, Ursula? I don't want you to change. I just want *you*."

Gripping the edge of the window sill, she looked out the window, and shook her head. "Please don't, Demetrio. I'm so confused."

He wanted to go to her, but she was trembling. He didn't want to prop her up, to hold her, to cover the confusion and fear. That wouldn't help her. "I know you are. I wish I could help, but I can't. It's up to you."

"I came to Italy to escape everything. I wanted nothing to do with Christmas, nothing to do with families, with celebrations. I wanted to be alone. And instead..." She shook her head wearily, and Demetrio's heart ached for this beautiful woman who had been so hurt that she had no idea what she felt anymore. And there was only one way to make her see beyond what had been so long entrenched in her personality, and it wasn't by prolonging the agony. Tough love. Wasn't that what it was called?

"Instead you found my family and me." He picked up his wallet from the coffee table and thrust it into his back pocket. Then he picked up his phone, turned it on and put it in his other pocket. "I can't do this anymore, Ursula. It's nearly time anyway, so let's leave for the airport now. You need to return to Sweden, and work out what it is you want because until you do, I don't want you here."

She looked up, and her eyes were full of hurt. "You said you loved me, but you don't want me here?"

"No." Every word he uttered which pushed her further away was breaking his heart, but he knew what she needed. And it wasn't for him to make things easy for her. "You have to understand. My wife was a wonderful woman, and she was very dear to me. But—and I've never told this to anyone, although my mother suspected—I never loved her as she loved me. And I think that hurt me more than it did her. I wouldn't wish that on anyone, least of all you. You come to me if, and when, you know for sure."

She nodded, and went toward her bags that were stacked by the door, her coat on top of them. They stood looking at each other. The despair was palpable, as was the need and longing. But there was nothing he could do to make it work. Only she could do that.

Suddenly the strident tone of the phone shattered the silence. As if awakening from a daze he answered it. "Hello!" Even as he spoke, his mind was full of Ursula, turning over the things he could say to her. Then he heard the hysterical tone in his sister's voice, and he immediately focused. "Marianna? Calm down. What is it?"

As he listened, he felt Ursula's touch on his shoulder. "What's happened?" No doubt she could hear Marianna's frantic voice.

He listened a few more minutes, calming Marianna as best he could. "You did the right thing. Don't worry about Nonna. Leave it to me."

"What's happened?"

He slipped the phone into his pocket and grabbed his jersey and coat. "*Accidenti*! Damn! Marianna's been trying to contact me, and I've only just turned on my phone. Car keys! Where the hell are the car keys?"

Ursula picked them up from behind a pot and handed them to him. "Can I help? Is it Nonna?"

"No, it's Lorenzo. He's had some kind of fit, and Marianna's on her way to the hospital. She's worried about leaving Carolina and Tomasso alone with Nonna because Papa has gone to see his sister in Siena and my mother isn't well enough to look after the kids. I have to go to Abbadia. But… Marianna is so upset."

"What about the neighbors?"

"Neighbors, Ursula? This is about family, not strangers." He glanced around the kitchen, but Ursula had already switched off the oven and lights. Then she turned him around, to face the door.

"Demetrio, go straight to the hospital and meet Marianna there. She needs you."

"But what about the kids? They'll be upset. If Marianna was like that, then the kids will be worse, and my mother is too weak to cope."

"I'll go to Abbadia. I'll look after them."

"But… your flight?"

"There'll be another one. And then another one after that. Go. Now."

Demetrio took her head in his hands and kissed her fiercely on the lips. He walked backward a few steps, loathe to leave behind that vision of bee-stung lips and surprised, wide eyes. But he had to, so he strode over to the door. "The keys to the Land Rover are in the bowl.

And a spare apartment key. Please, take them and lock up."

He didn't wait for an answer.

Ursula stood by the window for a few minutes watching Demetrio tear off, heading toward the hospital where his sister would soon be arriving. Then she grabbed her suitcase and bag and, took one last look around the apartment where she'd found such happiness, and slammed the door.

There was a certain irony, she thought, as she headed out of Florence onto the motorway that would take her the two-hour journey to Abbadia. Half an hour ago, she'd been about to run away from emotional attachment, and now, instead, she was returning to its heart. Italy obviously hadn't finished with her yet.

CHAPTER 9

Despite the time of day, the cars on the motorway had their headlights on because of the somber light. Ursula drove as fast as she dared in the unfamiliar car. As she drew closer to the mountains, freezing fog descended, and the lights from oncoming vehicles became diffuse, making visibility even more difficult, and reality seem even farther away. Ursula felt as if she were driving into a different world.

Demetrio rang periodically to see how she was progressing. Marianna had obviously driven like a woman possessed and was already at the hospital with Lorenzo, who was barely conscious with a high temperature and a rash over his little body. Ursula could hear Marianna crying in the background as Demetrio simultaneously comforted her while talking to Ursula.

Ursula knew how much his nephews and niece meant to Demetrio and she could hear the pain and fear in every syllable he uttered.

But Ursula was also struck by how Demetrio handled the stress of the situation. Unlike her last boyfriend, Demetrio was cool-headed and in control. When something had happened to her ex, he'd simply broken down. The man who could wheel and deal, who could broker multi-national agreements in corporate boardrooms, would become helpless if required to do anything practical, like take Ursula to hospital. But Demetrio's strength showed itself—like steel, becoming stronger when tested in the heat. He was focused, in control, and capable. She knew Marianna was in the best hands. And, equally, she knew that Demetrio would keep her company while she navigated the unfamiliar roads, which they'd traversed only days before in the other direction.

By the time she drove into the farmyard, it was dark. There were no outside lights on but inside, lights blazed at the windows, across which the curtains had only been roughly drawn. Of course, thought Ursula, Nonna wouldn't be able to draw the curtains from the top, and the children hadn't thought of it. She got out the Land Rover, slammed the door shut, and scrunched through the newly fallen snow toward the front door. Before she reached it, she heard shouts from inside, the door swung open wide, and Carolina and Tomasso came running through the snow in bare feet.

"Carolina! Tomasso! Inside straightaway, it's too cold!"

"Where's Mama?" demanded Tomasso.

"Where's Mama and Lorenzo?" gulped Carolina, her tear-stained face, distraught with worry.

"She's in hospital with Lorenzo making sure he's okay. Now, come on, let's get inside." She ignored Carolina's torrent of words, and Tomasso's quietly spoken, insistent ones, and put her arms around them both and swept them into the hall.

"Orsula?" came a worried voice from the kitchen. "Is that you?"

"*Si*, Nonna. I'm here."

"Thank goodness," said Nonna as Ursula entered the kitchen with the children. And Ursula thought she'd never forget the look of relief and welcome on the old lady's face. She felt as if she were coming home.

THE EVENING PROVED MORE arduous that she could ever imagine. Getting the children to calm down was bad enough, but Nonna was on the verge of collapse herself. It took all Ursula's negotiation skills to get the children fed and settled by the fire—which she had to make with the help of disjointed instructions from a worried Nonna. Then she had to sit and try to calm the old lady, whose intense frustration at being confined to a wheelchair didn't bring out the best in her. Things only really began to calm down after Demetrio's phone call.

Lorenzo was out of danger. The doctor had confirmed that it wasn't a case of meningitis as they'd feared, but a high temperature from a virus, combined with a food allergy. Now, it was a simple matter of waiting for the virus to run its course. Demetrio had wanted to know if she needed him there. But she'd insisted he stay with Marianna. She was fine.

She watched Nonna unload all her fears on Demetrio over the phone, and quieten as she listened to his reassuring responses. Demetrio seemed to carry the emotional burden for all the family, giving them the strength they needed to carry on. But what about him, Ursula wondered? How long could he continue to take it all on his shoulders, without refilling his reserves? With regret, she remembered the hurt in his eyes when she'd retreated from him. He was a strong man who'd opened himself up to her, and all she'd done was throw it in his face, because of her fears.

She only exchanged a few words with him over the phone. He'd wanted to know if she was okay; she was touched, but angry with herself at the same time. In addition to his fears about his nephew, he should ask how *she* was? She realized not just that Demetrio cared for her, but that she'd made herself appear weak in his eyes. And she wasn't weak, was she? So many questions and only she could come up with the answers.

IT WAS late afternoon the following day when Demetrio pulled up in front of the farmhouse. The outside light was on, and all the curtains were drawn against the cold. He turned off the engine and fell back against the seat for a few moments, suddenly aware of his exhaustion.

He'd been awake for thirty hours straight, not resting until his nephew was out of danger, and a bed had been found for Marianna beside her son. It had only been then that he'd allowed himself to leave them both and come to Abbadia. In addition to his worry about his nephew and Marianna, had been his concern for Ursula and how she was coping with his mother who, as dear as she was to him, wasn't the easiest of people to handle. And then there was also Carolina and Tomasso.

The difference between his world and hers had been so pronounced in Florence that he was worried how Ursula would cope in his family home. She wasn't used to the continuous demands of people on her time, energy, heart and mind. She was only used to looking after herself. Not that she was essentially selfish—he knew she wasn't—but how she would cope with the children and his mother, he had no idea.

He swept his hand through his hair and got out the car. The sound of the door closing, disturbed the quiet of the afternoon. It was strangely quiet, he thought, as he walked through the undisturbed snow to the front door of the farmhouse and pushed it open. He shook his head. No one had thought to lock the door. He doubted whether his mother could have even produced a key for Ursula.

He closed the farmhouse door behind him and braced himself for whatever he might find. But the hallway was quiet. A soft toy lay in the middle of the floor, at the bottom of the stairs. He picked up the much-loved knitted rabbit and walked into the kitchen. A quick glance revealed the fire was still alight. Just. He was surprised. He knew his mother was no longer able to manipulate the damper. He wondered if his father had returned home, but there was no sign of his car in the yard. Ursula must have managed to damp it down the night before, because getting the fire going from nothing was a skill in itself.

On top of the stove, a pot of stew was keeping warm. He lifted it. Simple food, but the aroma made his mouth water. The lunch things had been washed up and were draining on the side. Nobody but Nonna would know where everything went. Even he didn't. But a good attempt had been made, and most of the pots and pans had been hung up on the overhead rack where they belonged. The toy baskets were heaped up with children's toys, and the table had only its usual pile of papers, and the hand woven basket Marianna had made at school, which contained buttons, pins, and coins.

Despite his hunger, Demetrio left the kitchen without touching the food and went first to his mother's bedroom, knocked quietly and then entered. She appeared tiny in the large bed, which was topped with a quilt made from squares of material he remembered from various of his sisters' and mother's dresses over the years. He lingered there for a few moments, feeling the familiar stab of love and sadness that his mother was diminishing before his eyes. He closed the door quietly. The best thing his mother could do was to sleep while her grandson healed. When she awoke, he hoped he'd have even better news for her.

He walked along the landing to the children's rooms. They were empty of people but full of toys. It looked like Carolina and Tomasso had run riot in their rooms, but at least the chaos had been contained. But where were they? They couldn't have gone out, the Land Rover Ursula had used was still parked outside, now under several inches of snow.

Then he turned his steps toward Ursula's room. He frowned as he heard a murmur of voices. He didn't recognize any of them. What the hell?

The floorboards on the landing creaked as he hesitated outside. The door was slightly ajar, the voices were louder now and light spilled out onto the darkened landing. He knocked gently, his heart in his mouth. But there was no reply, only the constant murmur of voices.

He pushed the door open, and stopped and smiled at the sight before him. Ursula lay, fully clothed, on the bed. Unlike his parents' Spartan bedroom, Marianna had made sure the guest bedroom was furnished with a collection of feather pillows, and a goose-down duvet that was as warm as it was light. Marianna must have also supplied the pure white linen. It wasn't something his mother would have chosen. But it was exactly right for Ursula. Settled amongst the snowy-white linen, she lay fast asleep, with a child tucked under each arm. Books were strewn over the bed, with one having fallen over Ursula herself. As if worried she'd not be enough, there was also an audio book playing quietly in the background on her phone. The combination must have eventually sent them all to sleep.

Tomasso was neatly under the covers, curled under Ursula's arm. Carolina was untidily draped, half over Ursula with her other arm dangling over the edge of the bed. She took up most of the bed. Demetrio had to swallow a chuckle.

So, he thought, *this* is the woman who's too aloof to fit into our world?

He walked over to the nightstand and picked up her phone and was about to turn off the book when a new text lit the screen.

He frowned, about to replace the phone unread. Then something caught his eye. It was only much later that he realized what it was that made him fail to replace the phone. It was the word "require." Something inside him responded to that with anger. He glanced at the sleeping threesome and resolutely pressed the key that would reveal the whole message. That would be all he'd do, he told himself—just discover who it was who would dare to demand something of Ursula.

Ursula. You're expected at dinner on the 19th. Don't let me down. ETV will be there. A united family front is required.

He looked at Ursula and realized that, no matter how mature, how cool, how adult she appeared, she was still affected by a domineering mother who required Ursula to perform her part in her mother's world.

His heart went out to her. She didn't know it, but she'd just proved she could fit in and that she didn't need the approbation of a mother who only wanted her for superficial reasons.

He kicked off his shoes, stripped off his sweater and gently climbed into the bed beside them. Only Carolina turned, plopped her arm over Demetrio's chest, grinned sleepily and promptly fell back to sleep.

Demetrio felt that grin in the depths of his heart. He turned so he was facing Ursula, her profile illuminated by the light shining in from the landing. "Sweet dreams, Ursula," he whispered, content just to be close to her and the children whom he adored.

It was dark when Ursula finally awoke. She sat up with a start as she remembered she was responsible for everyone in the house. Nonna would need help, the kids would need feeding, and Lorenzo? She turned to pick up her phone to see if she'd received any messages from

Demetrio. She checked the time. It was six in the evening, and she suddenly realized she was unencumbered by children. She patted the dark bed. They'd gone. She turned on the light and cried out in surprise when she saw Demetrio lying on the other side of the bed, fast asleep.

She could hear the sound of the children's laughter coming from their rooms, where they'd obviously retreated to play with their toys. It was a miracle they hadn't woken her up. Carolina had obviously taken on board what Marianna had said to her, and had been acting remarkably responsibly for her age, for which Ursula would be eternally grateful. Then she turned to Demetrio.

Quietly she rose and went around to the other side of the bed and pulled the duvet over him. He didn't move. The hall light revealed his profile—a jawline chiseled through hard work and a determined character, and hair that was a fraction too long. No doubt he only went to the hairdressers when nagged by the female members of his family. And when they weren't around, he simply didn't notice. He had more important things to occupy his mind. Like keeping his world intact for future generations, like making sure his parents and siblings and their children were looked after. Like putting himself last.

She bent over and kissed him softly on the lips. She stayed there, eyes closed, breathing him in, wanting to absorb everything about him while she still could, allowing her to love him, for just those few moments when things were simple, when she could imagine, just briefly, that they had a future.

But that future was make-believe, and she pulled away to find Demetrio had opened his eyes and was watching her without moving.

"Demetrio! I didn't know you were awake."

His lips curved into a smile. "So you kiss only *sleeping* men, do you?"

"No, I… I mean, I—"

He reached up and put his hand on the nape of her neck, and pulled her down, close to his face once more. "Maybe you should prove you don't take advantage of sleeping men, by kissing an awake one?"

He cocked an eyebrow in query, and she began to laugh. He took shameless advantage of her weakened state by pulling her on top of him, putting his arms firmly around her so she couldn't move and kissing her until she didn't want to move.

His mouth sought hers in a hungry kiss, which showed nothing of the tension of the past day and a half, only release. Eventually, he let her pull away but not before he'd caressed her butt.

She shook her head. "I have only one word for you, Demetrio."

"Um, I'd like to know what that is," he said, his dark eyes revealing which way his thoughts were straying.

She licked her lips. "Children," she said, laughing, as he fell back on the bed with a sigh.

She rose, put on her shoes and walked over to the door, stopping only briefly to comb her hair and check her makeup. "Children," she repeated, "who have been very good. Listen to them now. I think Carolina is reading to Tomasso."

Demetrio smiled and swung his legs onto the floor. "You're right. We have a lot to do. But you'd divert the attention of a saint."

"I don't want to do that; I have no interest in saints."

She paused in the doorway, scared that if she turned around, her courage would fail her. And she wanted him to know. "No interest in anyone else really. Only you."

She walked quickly to the children's bedrooms. It was the first time she'd told him that he was important to her. It had seemed ridiculous after such a short time together to feel so much for someone. But she'd thought about what he'd said. How long did it take before you loved someone? Was there a set time? Nonna certainly didn't believe there to be a minimum time. She'd only just met her husband when she'd agreed to marry him. Some things were just right. But that was old Italy, and this was not. Life was more complicated now, no matter how much one felt for someone.

She took Carolina and Tomasso downstairs where she focused her attention on the fire which had died right down. She knew when Demetrio had entered the room before even the kids whooped and sprang on him. She felt her skin prickle under his brief gaze, before his attention turned to the children.

After he settled them down, he came to her. "Here, let me do that."

"You think I can't?" she asked softly, with a smile. The reaction to an offer of help was instinctive, no longer a real objection.

"I know you can. You've kept the fire going well. It's not easy."

"You sound surprised."

"I was."

She laughed. "So was I. I guess when you put your mind to something new, it's not as hard as one thinks."

"I guess you're right. And I guess that's true of pretty much every new situation."

He held her gaze, and she knew he was wondering if she'd changed her mind. She couldn't answer the unspoken question because she still didn't know.

She rose. "I'll go and check on Nonna and get dinner ready."

"Leave Nonna to me. You do what you have to do. Is…" He hesitated. "Is cooking a problem?"

"All I can say is thank goodness for Elisabetta's recipe books."

"Elisabetta…" Demetrio grunted with surprise, and walked to the door. He turned, and shook his head with a smile.

As he left the room and went toward his parents' bedroom, Ursula wondered how she could ever have *not* known this man. She smiled as she heard Nonna call out his name in delight.

After checking the children were okay, she busied herself getting dinner ready. She looked up as Demetrio brought Nonna into the living room in his arms. He placed her gently on the sofa and tucked a soft blanket around her. Ursula poured a cup of coffee and brought it over.

"Thank you." Nonna turned to Demetrio who sat down gratefully, looking exhausted. "I don't know what I'd have done without Orsula. She looked after little Carolina and Tomasso as if they were her own. Didn't you, Orsula?"

Ursula smiled. "I certainly tried."

Nonna petted Ursula's hand. "And you succeeded, *cara*. Now, Demetrio, tell me everything that happened. But before you do that, tell me how Lorenzo and Marianna are."

"Lorenzo is doing better than Marianna, to be truthful. He has bounced back much more quickly than her. She's exhausted. Thank goodness Vincenzo has arrived, although she still refuses to go home. But she has a bed in the hospital, and now that Vincenzo is there, she is resting."

"And what do they think caused the fit?"

"A virus. It's nothing too unusual, but combined with the rash, even the doctors were concerned."

Nonna crossed herself. "Thank the Lord that they are all well."

"And you? Have you all been okay? Did the children behave themselves?"

"They've been brilliant," said Ursula. "They've helped me, and looked after Nonna."

At the sound of the table being laid, the children came running in. Ursula handed them bowls of meat and vegetable stew and roughly sliced bread. They sat at the kitchen table, feet swinging, as Carolina sang a song between mouthfuls. It was a song which Ursula had taught her. Ursula looked at Demetrio who was frowning as he tried to decipher the words. She could tell the moment he understood. He smiled to himself, and Ursula busied herself with filling the sink with hot water.

"Do you want a hand, Ursula?" he asked.

"No, I'm fine. You must be exhausted. Rest."

"Go on," encouraged Nonna. "You go and help her. I'll keep an eye on these rascals."

"I'm not that tired," he said as he put his arm around

Ursula, and with the other, squirted dishwashing liquid into the sink.

"True. You wielded that dishwashing liquid like a fiend."

He grinned. "Tell me what else I can do to help."

"Seriously, just you being here is a great help. I mean, I managed, just, but it was quite a challenge at times."

"A challenge you rose to."

"Did you doubt it?"

He brushed his fingers against her cheek. "If I had any doubts I wouldn't have agreed with your suggestion to come here in the first place."

She kissed his fingertips. "Demetrio, you had no other choice."

"Well…" He grinned. "There is that."

"Are you two bringing me some cake, or do I have to stagger over myself to get it?" called Nonna, who had her back to them.

"Coming," called Ursula, flustered as she realized Demetrio's attention had made her forget she wasn't alone with him.

"You take those to the table," said Demetrio. "And I'll finish off here. Go on, you go and sit down."

When she hesitated, he rested his hands on her hips and brought her close to him, his nose brushing hers. "Go, because I want you less exhausted later."

She went because if she hadn't, she couldn't have answered for her actions.

Demetrio sat by the fire, half-listening to his mother as he reflected on what Ursula had said as she'd left the bedroom, about him being the only person she was inter-ested in. Had she had a change of heart?

He watched her as she moved around the kitchen, tidying up as if she belonged here. Why she couldn't see that she did belong here, was beyond him. Time meant nothing. One week, or one year, wouldn't change a thing. She *did* belong, and he only had a day in which to make her understand.

His attention was distracted by the two children whose play had become punctuated with over-tired squabbling. He rose and went to Ursula.

"Why don't you leave this to me, and take the children to bed. And then go to bed yourself." He could see faint traces of shadows under her eyes which hadn't been there before. She looked exhausted. "Okay?"

She stifled a yawn and wiped her hands on a towel. "Good idea." Ursula took the children's hands. "Come on, time for bed."

"I don't want to go," said Carolina.

"You can look through my makeup bag again if you like?"

"Okay," said Carolina, unable to resist such a treat.

"And, you, Tomasso, a story?"

Tomasso's thumb had already crept to his mouth, and he nodded approval. Demetrio watched them go.

"You like that girl don't you, Demetrio?" said Nonna, her eyes as penetrating as ever, but her lips curved into a gentle smile.

"Yes, I do. Very much."

He wheeled her to her bedroom.

"Have you asked her to marry you?"

"Of course not! We hardly know each other."

"That's nothing to do with anything. Look at your Papa and me. We knew immediately. Sure, there were things we had to work out. But who doesn't? It didn't change the fact that we knew, right from the start, that we were meant for each other."

Demetrio sighed. "It's not that easy. You and Papa were from the same culture, the same land; you shared the same point of view on everything. Ursula? Ursula is from a different world. Believe me, Mama, she's from a very different world."

Nonna made a puffing, dismissive sound, as Demetrio helped her into bed. "How different can it be? She's a woman; you're a man. You need to marry, come live here, and have babies. Life is simple if you don't complicate it."

Demetrio sighed once more. "Here's your medication. Do you want anything else?"

She reached out, and took his hand in hers. "Only one thing, my son. I wish to see you happy once more."

"I *am* happy, Mama."

She shook her head. It seemed he'd never be able to say enough to convince her.

He kissed her and left her with the light on, and a book at her side. But, as he turned to say goodnight, she hadn't moved and was still watching him. He smiled, blew her a kiss and closed the door.

With each step he took away from his mother, he knew she was right. Yes, he was content up to a point, but he couldn't live in the past anymore. He had to move on if he was ever to find true happiness. He stopped at the foot of the stairs to Ursula's room. One way led to his room, the other to hers. He looked up and saw her door was open. That was invitation enough for him.

He walked up to the open door and looked inside. He shook his head and laughed. Whatever he'd been hoping for, whatever he'd been expecting, his hopes were dashed, there and then, at the sight of Ursula fully dressed and fast asleep with two children either side of her. Tomasso had his eyes open and beckoned Demetrio inside.

Demetrio sighed and reckoned there was just about enough room.

CHAPTER 10

It was the clatter of pans from the kitchen below which awoke Demetrio. He lay for a few moments looking up at the whitewashed ceiling with the unfamiliar light fitting, then one of the children stretched, kicking Demetrio in the shin. He winced and turned to see Carolina smiling sleepily at him and Tomasso, just rousing from his sleep. Ursula was still out for the count. She must have been exhausted. His eyes lingered on her, amazed by her beauty. He reckoned he could look at her day in, day out, for years and never tire of her translucent skin, her lashes, and brows, a soft sable against her skin, now flushed with the heat of having two children draped around her.

But there was no time to admire her now. Carolina crawled across the bed, somehow not waking Ursula, kissed him and jumped down with a thud onto the rugs, hand woven by his grandmother. "I'm hungry."

Tomasso wasn't far behind her but lacked her coordination and tumbled to the floor with a crash before

Demetrio could catch him. Tomasso's grinning face showed he was none the worse for his fall.

"Hush," Demetrio said, bringing his finger to his lips, and indicating Ursula with his head. "Don't wake Ursula."

Carolina nodded, wide-eyed and important—not waking an adult, other than her parents, was something she'd never had to do before. It was always the younger children she shouldn't wake. Tomasso just looked at him. "Why?" he asked in a normal voice.

Demetrio groaned and glanced at Ursula, who merely shifted into a more comfortable position. Demetrio scooped up Tomasso and took him and Carolina outside. He gently closed the door. "Because, Tomasso, she's been busy with you guys all yesterday and last night, and deserves to sleep in."

Tomasso frowned as he absorbed Demetrio's explanation. "Nonna cried the night before you came!"

Demetrio closed his eyes briefly, saddened, at the thought of his stoic mother crying. "She was sad, Tomasso, and worried."

"About Lorenzo?"

"Amongst other things, yes."

"But Mama told us not to worry," said Carolina.

"And she was quite right. Worrying is for adults, not children. Now come on—let's go and have breakfast." If there was one thing Demetrio understood, it was the power of food to distract children. Tomasso ran off and perched on the landing, ready to jump from step to step. Demetrio grabbed him before he could. "And let's see how quietly we can go down the stairs." He pressed his finger to his lips, and Carolina did the same.

"Yes!" shouted Tomasso.

Demetrio winced, but no sound came from Ursula's room. He suspected she'd sleep through anything after a couple of days of caring for two confused and active kids, and one worried grandmother.

Once they managed to get downstairs without too much noise, he opened the door and ushered the children into the warm kitchen.

His mother had somehow managed to fire up the Aga and breakfast was already warming in the oven. *"Bon Giorno!"* she called out as she made caffè latte on the stove top.

Carolina and Tomasso wandered over to the basket of toys and started playing with the dolls.

Demetrio kissed his mother on the cheek. "Let me do that."

She batted him away. "I'm not dead yet. I've been making breakfast for fifty years, and I'm not going to stop now."

"Okay, you win." He took plates and cutlery and placed them on the table and sat down. "Have you heard from Marianna?"

"No," Nonna replied. "Marianna hasn't rung this morning yet. Have you heard any more news?"

"Just last night's text saying Vincenzo would come by to pick up the children early this morning. He should be here soon."

"Ursula helped pack their things. To be honest, Demetrio, I would have been lost without her. The kids were inconsolable. You know how worked up Marianna gets. It had rubbed off on the kids, as usual, and they were practically hysterical."

"She had reason to be. The last time Lorenzo got this sick, he was hospitalized for weeks."

Nonna grunted assent, and Demetrio knew she felt more than she was expressing. It was her way, and the way of her parents before her to be stoic in the face of adversity. "Well, thank God for Ursula, because she managed to settle them down."

Demetrio followed his mother's gaze to where the two children sat cross-legged on the home-made rag rug, their dolls between them.

"I'll be the legal counsel today," Tomasso said.

"You were the legal counsel yesterday."

"But legal counsels have more fun!"

"Let's have two then."

Satisfied, they continued their game.

Demetrio turned to his mother. "Since when has Barbie been a legal counselor?"

"Since Ursula decided she would be." Nonna turned to Demetrio, raised an eyebrow and chuckled. "I heard her telling Carolina that Legal Counsellor Barbie had more fun than Beach Barbie and that she also wore better clothes. And Ursula certainly knows how to dress a Barbie."

Demetrio snorted and took the tray of warm pastries from his mother. "Kids, come and have some food."

"Ursula should stay. Have you told her to stay?" asked Nonna.

"I can't *tell* her to stay, Mama. I've asked her, yes. But it's up to her, and she's determined to leave as soon as she can."

Nonna shook her head, and turned her attention to making sure the children ate their breakfast.

They'd just finished eating when Marianna's husband, Vincenzo, arrived on a wave of cold air. After the greetings were over, he accepted a quick espresso, and updated them on Lorenzo's progress. Lorenzo was recovering as quickly as he'd declined. It seemed it was a combination of a virus and a food allergy which had confused the diagnosis. He'd be fine within a few days. Probably in better health than either parent, his father conceded. Meanwhile, the family was cutting short their stay in Abbadia San Alexis and returning to Florence.

But the children refused to leave without saying goodbye to Ursula. Demetrio agreed, providing Ursula was awake. He allowed Carolina to creep into her room. Whether she was awake or was awoken, Ursula emerged, pulling her hair back into a ponytail.

"Demetrio! How's Lorenzo? Carolina tells me he's recovering. Is that so?"

"He's much better. Vincenzo is here to take the kids home. They wanted to say goodbye to you first."

Tomasso greeted Ursula with a big hug at the bottom of the stairs. After more cuddles, and promises of phone calls and postcards from Sweden, the children disappeared out the door with their father.

Demetrio wheeled his mother back into the hall. "I need a rest, Ursula, so I'll say goodbye to you now," said Nonna. "Demetrio tells me you plan to return to Sweden today. Safe travels."

Ursula looked from Demetrio back to Nonna. "Thank you. I've rebooked my flight for this evening. I have work to do, so…"

"So you must return. I understand. Now"—she indicated for Ursula to bend down and Nonna kissed her—

"don't be a stranger to us. Come again. You know you'll always be welcome."

Ursula took Nonna's hands. "Thank you so much for everything."

Demetrio stepped away, watching the two of them say goodbye as if they were mother and daughter, not two women who had only known each other for just over a week.

Nonna took hold of Ursula's face between her two hands and swept her thumbs down her cheeks. "Look after yourself, Ursula. And do what you think right."

Demetrio closed the door behind his mother. "Would you like to go for a walk?"

Ursula drained her coffee. "Definitely."

As he closed the back door behind them and they strode out across the icy field toward the woodland, Demetrio looked at her curiously. "What did Nonna mean, 'and do what you think right?'"

"Hm?" asked Ursula with a slight smile.

"You heard me, Ms. Adamsson. Have you been having tête-à-têtes with my wise mother?"

"And if I have?"

He shrugged and kept his eye on the rocky outcrop of the hill above the treetops, a smudge of charcoal in all the white. "Then I imagine that you're lucky to receive her wise words. She certainly offers them freely enough to her children. I don't see why we should be the only ones to suffer!"

Ursula laughed. "Demetrio! As it happens, she did as much listening as talking. She's a wonderful woman. You're very lucky."

He reached out and took her hand, and felt her

answering grip with satisfaction. "I know. And I thank God for my family every day."

They entered the woods where the silence was denser somehow, with everything muffled by snow. A bird took off from a branch above their heads, showering snow on their upturned faces. Ursula laughed, but Demetrio didn't. He looked down at her and brushed off the snow from her nose. "You're the proverbial ice queen—so beautiful, so cool."

Her smile fled instantly. "Don't say that, Demetrio. I don't like to think I'm cold."

"I didn't mean you're cold in your heart. I *know* you're not."

"*I* don't know that. And that's what scares me. Demetrio, I was taught *not* to feel, I was taught to hide everything. And I was always a good student."

She turned away, as if embarrassed and touched a tree, the snow barely holding together, dripping to the forest floor, its warmth creating a hole in the snow.

He followed her gaze. "It's thawing. The worst is over. For now, anyway. It could all be gone by tomorrow."

"I can't imagine this land without snow." She looked up at him. "It's been magical, Demetrio. Simply magical."

"But you won't consider staying."

"As you said yourself, this will be gone soon. It's just a moment. Just a perfect moment."

"I'm not so cynical as to believe that a perfect moment can't lead to another, and then another."

"I'm cynical now, am I?"

"Yes. You're cynical, and you're afraid."

"Hm," she said, trailing her gloved hand across a snowy branch. "So many bad things, it's a wonder I survive."

"Not bad. Just sad. And, no doubt, you believe these traits are the reason you survive; they are your defense mechanisms against the world."

She paused, studying the snow as if her life depended on it. "Please, Demetrio, don't."

"Don't what? Tell the truth?"

She turned to him, her beautiful face suddenly flushed with anger. "Don't think you know me based on the limited time we've spent together, because you don't."

She began to walk away, but he caught up and took hold of her hand. "Wait, please. Just listen for a moment. You're right. But because I don't know the whole of you doesn't mean that I don't know a few parts of you. And important parts as it happens. And that doesn't come from what's been said; it comes from *how* it's been said; it comes from *glances*, from things that no one can prove, no one can replicate. It comes from how I feel for you." He took her hand and held it against his stomach. "I feel you, here, viscerally, in the pit of my stomach."

She smiled. "Not your heart?"

"Everywhere."

"I can't, Demetrio. It's too much, too soon. I have to leave."

He looked away. "Of course. I don't wish to argue. Let's continue our walk. It's your last afternoon here. I take it you're still catching the flight tonight?"

She nodded. "Yes. I love it here, Demetrio. Truly. But I'm not sure that's the same as moving here."

"In that case, you must go. Return to Sweden. But then you must come here again, for another holiday. And then another." His grip on her arm tightened.

She bit her lip, and turned away.

Demetrio released her arm. He didn't expect a reply. "We'd better get going," he said. "It's nearly time."

Time for Ursula to go. Time for the fledgling dreams that had begun to grow inside—fighting their way through the sadness that had held his heart captive for so long—to fly away too.

DEMETRIO AND URSULA made only one stop, and that was to his apartment to collect her suitcase. She hadn't even wanted to come in. She'd already moved on.

Demetrio was silent as Ursula made small talk on their way from his apartment to the airport. How could she say such inconsequential things after what they'd shared was about to end?

They parked, and he got out and retrieved her bag for her. They walked in silence toward the airport. He'd ask her. He had to ask her because who knew if he'd see her again? He pressed the elevator button in the car park and turned to her. "Ursula, I—"

But the elevator doors opened, revealing a big noisy Italian family with more bags than people. For once, Demetrio wished his countrymen weren't quite so all-consuming and conspicuous. He and Ursula squashed in beside them.

"Yes?" asked Ursula.

He cleared his throat and shook his head, unwilling to raise his voice and say what he had to say with an audience. "Nothing. It can wait." But he knew that the waiting time had nearly run out.

He held her back as the others emerged from the

elevator. They walked out onto the departure concourse, and Ursula looking around, trying to see where to place her bags. "It's over there."

"Ursula." It was now or never. People milled around them, but they stood, unmoving, in the mêlée. "Ursula, I need to ask you something."

She frowned. Could she really have no idea what he was about to say? "Sure. What is it?"

He cleared his throat again. "I want to know if—"

"Ursula!" Suddenly a crowd of Ursula's friends descended on them. It was Ruby and some of the others they'd met at the jazz club. Ruby embraced Ursula who was suddenly all smiles, smiling more than she had all day. It made Demetrio realize that she was happier to see them, than she had been in his company. He took a step back, glad that he'd been stopped from saying what he'd been about to say, glad that he'd been prevented from making a fool of himself.

"You didn't think we'd let you slip away without us seeing you, did you?" asked Ruby laughing. She turned to Demetrio. "Hi, again!"

He nodded.

"I thought you'd still be partying," said Ursula.

"We are. We just brought the party to you. Come on! Let's go to the café."

They swept Ursula along. The chatter moved swiftly from the personal, to people they knew who'd appeared in gossip columns, to who was in the latest movies. Demetrio shook his head as he followed behind. How the hell could she put up with such inane chatter? This wasn't the Ursula he knew. And then he remembered, when things became too personal, when she was most scared, she'd retreat into small talk. He suddenly understood.

Ursula glanced at Demetrio and shrugged, as they piled in around a table. Demetrio placed her suitcase on the floor beside her, and remained standing.

"I'd better be going now."

Ruby looked from Demetrio to Ursula, and then back to Demetrio. "No, don't go," said Ruby. "Sit here with us, and tell us about yourself. We didn't get to chat last time we met."

"I'm not much of a talker. Besides, there's nothing much to tell."

Ursula's friends looked at him in surprise before looking back at Ursula, obviously curious to see what her response would be. To them, this was all some kind of game. But Ruby appeared oblivious to her companions' curiosity and, refusing to be denied, patted the seat beside her. Ursula sat on her other side. Demetrio sat down, purely because he couldn't face leaving Ursula yet.

Ruby's friend pulled a face. "I guess you're right, Demetrio, is it? There's nothing much to tell because nothing happens in the country, does it?" She turned to Ursula. "You'll be glad to get back into the real world, then, Ursula. Has it been awful stuck in the country with nothing going on? Poor you."

Ursula shook her head. She looked as if she was about to speak, but after a glance at Demetrio, she said nothing.

"You're polite because Demetrio's here. But you don't mind our teasing, do you Demetrio?" the woman continued.

It seemed a response wasn't required and no one saw his glare as the conversation started up again, batting quick fire, back and forth. It was like a tennis volley, Demetrio thought. Smashing words back and forth, the winner finding the sweet spot, the punchline, regardless of who was hurt. In fact, the harder it hit, the harder the subsequent laughter.

Having begun the conversation, Ruby sat back, as if she'd done what she had to do, got the ball rolling and left it up to everyone else to entertain, or not. Ursula had told him something of Ruby's background. She needed people and activity around her at all times. Well, she had that now. And so did Ursula, who was also not speaking. Not listening, either, if he'd learned anything about her.

After having seen the kind of friends she had he could just imagine the life she led, and how different it was to his—it was like comparing night to day. And he had a strange feeling that that was just what Ursula wanted to show him.

"So, tell me all about your Christmas," said Ruby's friend to Ursula. "I really can't imagine you in a rural farmhouse. Was it primitive?"

"No!" Ursula hesitated. "No, of course not." Another glance at Demetrio. "It was… traditional."

They laughed as if she'd told a joke. She shook her head again, in denial, but not denying it with any words.

Demetrio felt betrayed. He stood up, and the conversation stopped. He looked beyond Ruby to Ursula. "Why are you doing this, Ursula?"

"Doing what?"

"You *know* what. You're betraying me, and my family, by not defending my life against their jokes."

The others tried to smother their laughter, but Ruby wasn't laughing and nor was Ursula.

Ursula rose, too. "I don't mean to, Demetrio. You and your family have been wonderful to me. But it's like I've been saying, my world is different to yours." She shrugged. "It's just the way it is."

"And it's the way you want it to be."

"It's the way it *has* to be." She paused. "It's what I want," she added.

The others looked at each other entranced by the scene playing out before them. Ruby rose. "Tell you what, I'll get more drinks!" She walked away as if either she couldn't cope with the emotional scene, or she truly thought another round of drinks would fix everything.

He shook his head, his gaze firmly fixed on Ursula. "No. You haven't the courage to take what you want, and I don't want to share my life with someone who doesn't have courage."

He wanted to reach out and grab her, to take hold of her so she could never leave him, to throw her over his shoulder and carry her off into the snow and wilderness and just be alone with her.

He heard another smothered, awkward giggle and he stepped back. He wasn't going to give these people any more reasons to laugh at him.

Instead, he turned away, and it felt like he was tearing himself in two. He didn't look back, just kept on walking toward the automatic doors through which people moved like waves, ebbing and flowing, back and forth, forever going and returning but never getting anywhere. But not him. He knew what he wanted, even if no one else did. And right now, he couldn't have it, so he needed to get out and, more than anything, not look back.

. . .

Ursula watched Demetrio walk away.

She wanted to call out to him, go running after him, stop him from taking another step away from her. She felt as if some connection was being stretched to breaking point.

She should have said something, defended the world that he loved so much, but she hadn't. And she knew why. He believed her to be capable of fitting in. He thought she was a homemaker, someone who could live a traditional life with him. But she wasn't. She'd never lived like that before, and she didn't know if she could do it. What if she risked everything to find she had nothing to give?

And what better way to get the message across to him, than this. He hadn't believed anything she'd said. Maybe he'd believe something she *hadn't* said.

"Ursula!" Ruby joined them with another bottle of Champagne. "And I've beer for Demetrio." She looked around. "Where's he gone?"

"He had to go home." She bit her lip. "He'd hardly want to stay with us demolishing all the things which mean so much to him." She could hardly contain her tears. The others looked uncomfortable and took solace in their drinks, resuming their talk about some magazine debacle. It seemed that death and disaster were the only things which absorbed her friends. She hadn't noticed it before.

Only Ruby looked at her with sympathy. Ruby clung to her superficial world as if for survival. Ursula knew some of her past but, she suspected, not all of it. Now, as Ruby took hold of her hand and squeezed it, with a heart-felt look of sympathy in her eyes, she knew that she was different.

"I'm sorry, Ursula. We shouldn't have said those things. When people lead lives so different to my own, lives I don't really understand, it unnerves me, makes me say things I shouldn't. I'm so sorry if we drove Demetrio away."

"It wasn't you. It was me. I should have defended him and his world. I should—" Ursula's voice cracked, and she couldn't continue.

"Go," said Ruby. "Go and find him and tell him how you feel."

"That's just it. I don't *know* how I feel. And even if I do, I don't know if that's enough."

"It looks like it is, from where I was sitting."

Ursula swiped her fingers under her eyes. She rose and half-walked, half-ran toward the exit. She stepped outside onto the concourse opposite where the cars descended from the car-park, just in time to see Demetrio's car emerge and pass in front of her. He didn't look around. She doubted he'd seen her. But she felt him go, deep inside. The stretch and pull of the connection they'd forged in the mountains, extended beyond its strength and broke.

CHAPTER 11

One month later...

"The Caribbean was too crowded. I told Edward that it'll have to be the Maldives next year."

Ursula cringed inwardly and glanced at the too thin, too tanned woman—a friend of her mother's—as she performed in front of a group of friends. Before Christmas, Ursula wouldn't have turned a hair, wouldn't even have noticed anything was amiss. But that was before she'd met Demetrio. Now, as she looked around at the glittering crowd, its glossy exterior could no longer hide its superficiality, not when she saw everything through Demetrio's eyes.

Ursula picked up a glass of Champagne from a passing waiter and walked over to the picture windows that overlooked Stockholm city center with its beautiful ochre and red buildings, surrounding an icy harbor. She knew the city lay before her but it was mid-winter and dark now and all she could see was herself—blonde hair gleaming, long black gown clinging in all the right places. She looked the part. Why didn't she feel it?

She turned around, leaned back against the window, and saw her friend Ruby, surrounded by a group of admirers. Ruby had joined Ursula in Stockholm shortly after she'd left Florence. Ruby was looking relaxed and happy, as she re-told some anecdote or the other.

Ursula smiled. She loved Ruby, and their recent late night conversations had helped Ursula to see things more clearly. They'd been good friends since they'd met five years ago at a party. Ruby had just begun to model at that time and had been an instant success, with her beauty, fun-loving personality and outspokenness. But Ursula knew the real Ruby—the woman who'd nursed a heartache over the past seven years that gnawed away inside her. Ursula thought she was looking a little too thin —good for a model, maybe, but for Ruby? Ursula worried about her.

"Ursula!" She turned to see her handsome friend Robert, who'd been circling her over the past few months, much like a shark hunting its prey. He stood directly in front of her, blocking her view of the rest of the room. "You weren't around this Christmas. Where have you been hiding?"

"Hiding? Yes, I guess you could call it that. Life before Christmas seems a long time ago."

"It was a month ago."

"A lot can happen in a month." She sighed. A lot could change, a lot could come to you, and a lot could be left behind.

He shrugged, as he considered what she'd said. "True. Stock markets can plummet or rise within hours. I can't let a day go by without checking my investments. There's always something to be bought or sold." He rocked back on the heels of his leather-soled shoes. "Can't leave it to my investment managers. You've always got to keep an eye on things yourself. Take oil, for example…"

Ursula let him drone on. She'd stopped listening the moment he'd given that self-satisfied rock back on his heels. She'd known men like him all her life, and she was tired of them, bored with what they talked about, irritated by their smugness, and essentially, repelled by their lack of substance. It was all about money. Nothing else mattered. But it did to her, now.

"Would you like to, Ursula?"

She jerked her head up. "Sorry, what?"

"I was just saying that I'm about to flick off some of my commercial property in Manhattan and I'm looking to reinvest in Miami. Prices are still strong there. I wondered if you'd like to come along for the ride?"

She shrugged, as she briefly wondered how long her attention had strayed for him to move from oil to Miami in such a short time. Probably not long. All he ever talked about was money.

"So, how about it?"

"Er, no, sorry. I've no plans to travel to the States anytime soon."

He grinned. "Then make some."

Her smile fixed, and she looked around, trying to work out how she could leave him without appearing rude. She caught Ruby's eye. "No. I won't be going to the States. I have other plans. I have a lot on with work." She added, hoping that would stop him.

He shrugged. "Maybe later, then."

Apparently it took more than a hint to stop the advances of a self-absorbed man.

"Robert!" said Ruby appearing like a guardian angel. Ursula sighed with relief. "How nice to see you again." They exchanged pecks on the cheek. "Have you been entertaining Ursula?" Ruby grinned at Ursula.

"I've just been telling her about how well my property portfolio is doing."

"Oh, lovely." Ruby smiled with great charm. "I'm sure she was fascinated. Did she tell you where she's just been?"

Robert tried to look interested. "No, where?"

"Italy." She took a sip of her Champagne.

"Oh, I was in Milan recently. Some friends of mine have just bought a villa on Lake Como." He grimaced. "It's not the optimum time to buy. Now, if he'd—"

"No," interrupted Ruby. "Ursula was staying in the country." She gave Ursula a knowing smile.

"The country?" said Robert. It was all Ursula could do not to laugh. He might as well have been told that she'd gone to the moon for the weekend. "Surely not? You must have been close to a city?"

Ruby pulled a face and shook her head. "The house was miles from its next neighbor, would you believe?"

"No, I wouldn't," he said, looking at Ursula in alarm.

"Well, it's true."

"Why would you go to the country?" asked Robert. "There's nothing there."

"Ursula?" said Ruby, with her butter-wouldn't-melt-in-her-mouth expression.

Ursula sighed. "I got lost, and then liked it, and stayed for a while. End of story."

"Got lost in the country? With nothing but fields and trees, and things."

"There *are* people there, too, you know," Ursula said.

"But what kind of people?" He snorted. "Not *our* kind, surely."

"Well, *my* kind. Not sure if they're yours or not."

"If they're country bumpkins, yokels, simple folk who do the same thing day in, day out, year after year, then true, they're not my sort. And they don't sound like yours, either, Ursula."

"How so?" Ursula knew what he meant, but his comment irked her.

"You know. The kind of people who live in these places, lead very *small* lives. Stuck in weird, crumbling houses, living in the past, doing the same-old, same-old. God, it would drive you crazy!"

"You mean it would drive *you* crazy."

"Same thing."

"I don't think so," she said quietly.

Robert raised his eyebrow as if he suddenly twigged what was happening. "Oh, I see." He swirled his drink and then looked back up at her. Ruby and Ursula exchanged glances. "You know, it's purely novelty value. All that"—he waved his hand in the air—"getting back to nature stuff. Sure, it has its appeal. Some of those old farmhouses, given major overhauls, smarten up real nice for country retreats. But that's all it is, you know, Ursula. A retreat from the real world. There's nothing there. Nothing happens. Just the same as what's gone on for centuries."

"And is that so bad? There's a lot to be said for tradition, for celebrating with family, for being there for each other in times of need, and in times of happiness."

"Family?" he scoffed. "How often do you spend time with your family?"

"Not often enough. You're right. But I aim to correct that."

"I'll believe *that* when I see it." He laughed again. "I can just picture it! Ursula, slaving over a hot Aga."

"It has been known," she replied quietly, remembering the time it had taken to restart the Aga in the morning. The trips to the woodshed, the feeding of the wood chips, one by one into the fire pit, coaxing it into sullen life. What was the point in trying to make someone like Robert understand?

"An Aga?" He shook his head. "You're mad. This"—Robert waved his glass, indicating the rest of the room—"is your natural habitat. Networking, making deals, connecting with people."

"Maybe it *was*, but not anymore." He hadn't a clue, and she couldn't help but feel sorry for him, with his money-obsession, with his surety and smugness that *his* lifestyle was superior to all others. "I'm leaving it behind. I'm—"

Just then her cell phone beeped. If she'd been talking to anyone else, she'd have ignored it. But Ruby had been caught up elsewhere, and she desperately needed an excuse to end the conversation.

"Excuse me." She pulled her phone from her purse and checked the text. It was from Demetrio. She could have sworn her heart stopped. She glanced up at Robert who was still hovering, watching her. "I, I have to deal with this. Sorry!"

She walked away and then checked her phone once more. She hadn't heard from Demetrio since her return. She'd tried to phone him to apologize for what had happened at the airport, but she hadn't been able to leave a message, not when hearing his voice had caught her off-guard, and brought a lump to her throat. She'd got as far as, "It's Ursula, I'm…" but hadn't been able to find the words to express what she wanted to say, and had ended the call. She'd thought that maybe he'd phone her back, but he hadn't returned her call, until now.

She scrolled through the text, but there was only one line.

Do you like surprises?

She paused, frowned, and then began to text with shaking fingers.

Only good ones.

Her heart was pounding as she focused intently on the phone. What was this all about? Why now? Had something happened to Lorenzo again? Had something happened to Nonna, or Demetrio himself? She paced toward an alcove, needing to be away from all of these people, to focus on the one person whose messages she'd imagined—she'd dreamed of—every waking moment since she'd left him. She almost jumped as the text came through and its vibration traveled up her arm.

Turn to the door and text me if it's a bad one, and the surprise will disappear. If it's a good one, then…

Ursula turned before she'd finished reading his text and saw Demetrio, standing alone by the door, still wearing his coat, hair wet from the snow, looking straight at her with an expression in his dark eyes that shot straight to her heart.

Her phone slipped through her fingers and hit the parquet floor with a clatter. She walked swiftly to him, pushing or weaving around groups until she found herself standing in front of him, somehow breathless even though she'd only walked across the room.

She couldn't speak immediately, just devoured him with her eyes. With his height and dark good looks, he easily fitted into this room of beautiful people. But there was something which set him apart. It could have been the casual way he was dressed—black trench coat that had seen better days, worn jeans and a black sweater underneath. Certainly, none of the people in the room would have seen dead in clothes which were not in pristine condition. But it wasn't only this which made him stand out. It was his air of indifference, of confidence in himself that drew her like a moth to a flame. She wanted to be warmed by that flame so desperately. She ached to touch him.

"Demetrio." She reached out to him, to reassure herself that he was real, then stopped herself. "Is it really you?"

His smile was real enough. "It is. Good surprise, or bad?"

She didn't manage to contain her grin. "Good. Definitely good." But while her body felt energized just being near him, her mind had turned to mush. "But, what..." The question hung between them. There was so much she wanted to know, and so much she had no right to know, not after what she'd said and done.

"What am I doing here? I've come to see you, of course. Why else would I be in Stockholm?"

Her heart pounded, hardly daring to believe he was here to see her. "I don't know. Business? Scandinavia has some interesting landscape architects. Maybe..."

He shrugged. "I can say that if it's easier for you to accept."

She shook her head. How could she hope to protect herself from this man? "It's just that…"

"You're afraid."

She nodded. "And I'm so sorry—about all the things I said." She paused. "Or didn't say…"

"Hm. You certainly didn't leap to my defense, or that of my family, or our way of life. But then, I was hardly very understanding, was I? I didn't listen to you properly; I didn't give you enough time to adjust. I was too demanding, and you backed off."

"And you're being way too reasonable as well, Demetrio. What I did, and didn't say, was so wrong of me. I think, in some way, I wanted you to believe the worst of me. I wanted you to see, with your own eyes, why I wouldn't fit in."

"Why would you want to do that?"

"Because you wouldn't believe me when I told you I didn't belong in Italy, with you."

"Right."

It was all he said, but she could see that there was no change in his eyes. He held her gaze steadily, as if able to see through her defenses, through her self-delusion, to the heart of things.

The room suddenly felt airless. Everyone else, apart from Demetrio, had dissolved into an amorphous back-ground, inconsequential and irrelevant.

Suddenly a tray appeared between them, laden with glasses of Champagne. "Champagne, sir, madam?" asked the waiter.

They both shook their heads, and the waiter moved on.

But the moment had passed and Ursula stepped away

abruptly. Why was he here? *Really*. "And how is Lorenzo? Is he fully recovered?"

"He's fine. It's as if nothing had ever happened. He's bounced back and is now creating havoc for Marianna back home."

"And your parents?"

"Papa is well. My mother is sad though. She'd hoped you'd return for Twelfth Night and, when you didn't, she charged me with coming to give you your present myself."

Ursula swallowed. "Oh." She couldn't hide the disappointment. "*Nonna* sent you here?"

"Yes. She told me what I knew already. She told me that you were afraid and that I had to help you." He laughed uncomfortably. "I don't know what makes old women so damned wise."

"Maybe the fact that they're old… and they're women," she added with a smile.

"True." He smiled, and it lit up his face. She felt it wriggle its way deep inside her, warming her as nothing else could. "And that's fine, that you're afraid. It just means that other people have to be less afraid."

"Other people?"

"Me, of course, I mean *me*. If you're afraid, then I have to have the courage for both of us if we're to move forward."

He reached for her hand and brought it to his lips. Then he studied it as if it were the most interesting thing he'd ever seen and dropped a kiss on her palm. Then he folded it tightly within his. It was all she could do to concentrate on what he was saying, as she struggled to contain her response to his lips on her hands.

"To move forward?" she repeated.

"Otherwise, I fear, if I left it to you, we'd both continue to live in fear, in the past, unable to move forward, unable to break through that safety net we've both woven around ourselves."

That caught her attention. "*You*, afraid? I don't believe you're afraid of anything."

"Then you'd be wrong. I'm afraid of change. I'd keep everything the way it is, now, and forever, if I could—with my land, and my family. But I can't. My parents won't live forever. Things are always changing, whether I like them to or not. *You* made me realize that."

At that moment Ruby and a frowning Robert came up to them. "Demetrio!" Ruby kissed him on both cheeks. "What a lovely surprise." She looked from Ursula whose cheeks burned, back to Demetrio. "And what brings you here?"

Was it Ursula's imagination or had news that the ice queen, Ursula Adamsson, was holding hands with a strange Italian, spread through the whole room? People had begun wandering toward them.

"Sweden is beautiful, Ruby. But it's Ursula who brings me here, of course."

His words were heard by about a dozen people who now pressed around them. Ursula was aware of their mutterings, the repetition of her name, but had no idea what they were saying. All she could focus on was Demetrio.

Ruby was the only one who seemed to have her wits about her. Ursula looked at her with pleading eyes, and Ruby responded. "Absolutely understandable, of course, Demetrio. I'm here because of Ursula too."

"She's a popular person."

Ursula opened her mouth but couldn't find any words.

Ruby grinned. "A very popular person, even when she has nothing to say."

Ursula cleared her throat. "Demetrio is here because his mother asked him to bring me something."

"Interesting," Ruby said, looking from one to the other, a smile playing on her lips. "Just as well you've come now, Demetrio, because tomorrow you'd have missed her."

Demetrio turned with a stunned expression to Ursula, shaking his head in disbelief. "You're leaving? But you've only just arrived."

"That's what I said to her." Robert moved forward to shake Demetrio's hand. "It's work, work, work, with Ursula. I told her to let it wait until the holiday season is over. But she reckons this is too important."

"Work…" Demetrio repeated faintly. Then he shook his head as if shaking off a dream. "You're leaving for work reasons."

"Yes, work. But—"

"But, nothing!" Robert said. "You work too damn hard, Ursula. She won't even come to the States with me!"

Demetrio's expression changed instantly. He took a step toward Robert, and Ursula gave a little cry as Ruby, who must also have seen the effect of Robert's words on Demetrio, stepped between him and Robert.

Ruby smiled. "Robert won't give up hope, despite Ursula's constant rejections." They turned to Robert who looked stunned by this news and Demetrio's stance relaxed a little. "Demetrio, you should ask Ursula about her new job. She's quite passionate about it, you know."

"You didn't mention you've got a new job, Ursula," said

Robert, who didn't appear to notice that he'd been soundly defeated in the previous conversation.

"A new job?" asked Demetrio. "Oh." He looked uncertainly at the exit as if wondering how he could make his escape. He glanced at her with a small smile that was as brief as it was slight. "So, you're starting something new. That's good."

"Yes, I needed to do something. After Christmas, so…"

"Demetrio!" Some acquaintance of Demetrio's pushed through the thickening crowd and extended his hand to his. "Good to see you, again. We met at the design conference in Milan last year. What brings you to Stockholm?"

If Demetrio remembered the man, or even heard the question, he showed no sign. He didn't take his eyes off Ursula, and his expression cut her to the quick. There was a pain there which she felt in her own body. She fisted her free hand, rubbing her knuckles with her fingers to try to take away the pain. It didn't work, and she knew the only thing that would work, would be to take away the pain from those beautiful chestnut brown eyes.

She wanted to hold his head firmly in her hands, and kiss him. But before she could make a move, Demetrio's acquaintance pushed through and thrust his hand in front of Demetrio. Demetrio ignored it again. But the man wasn't going to be put off easily. "What brings you to Stockholm, Demetrio?" he repeated.

"Why am I here?" He shrugged and looked down at Ursula's hand that he still held in his. He pressed his lips together regretfully and dropped her hand and took a step away. "I'm not sure."

"Demetrio!" Ursula reached out for his hand and grabbed it tightly. As she tried to mold the chaos of words and thoughts and feelings which spun around her mind, into some tidy semblance of meaning, she watched Demetrio's expression change. His lips curved slowly into a smile that lit his eyes. She might have been tongue-tied at that moment, unable to express everything that fought to be expressed, but it seemed he understood anyway.

"Why am I here? I'm here to tell Ursula that I love her."

Her gasp was only surpassed by that of the crowd who turned as one to look at her. She licked her lips, as words still refused to form. Luckily it seemed Demetrio, unlike Robert, didn't need plain speech to understand something. He had something much rarer, an empathy which allowed him to understand her, when she hardly understood herself.

"And I've come here to persuade her to marry me," Demetrio continued. "With this ring." He brought a small antique velvet box from his pocket and opened it. "It belonged to my grandmother. Ursula, when I told my mother I wanted to marry you, she said you should have this."

"Ursula?" A laughing Ruby tugged at her arm. "Now is so *not* the time to be tongue-tied."

"Marry you?" Robert asked abruptly. "That's a bit sudden, isn't it? You two hardly know each other. What was it, Ursula? A month, did you say?"

Ursula licked her lips and swallowed. "Twelve days, seventeen hours and twenty-four minutes."

"I rest my case," Robert said. "That's not long."

"Long enough," said Ursula. She sucked in a deep breath. "It's long enough for me to know where I want to be; long enough for me to buy into a community law practice in Abbadia San Alexis. Long enough for me to know that I'd risk everything to return to Abbadia, knowing I have to be near Demetrio, whether he wants me or not. Long enough for me to know where I need to be."

Demetrio pulled her to him. "Come home, Ursula."

She nodded. "Yes."

He slid his hands up through her hair and, holding her head gently in his hands, he brought her face to his and kissed her. To much applause and cheering, they continued to kiss, and Ursula never wanted it to end.

EPILOGUE

Eleven months later

Ursula slammed the car door shut and stood for a moment in the farmyard. Snow had begun to fall. It had arrived late this year. She wondered how her life would have turned out if the snow had delayed this time last year. It didn't bear thinking about. Her phone vibrated, and she plucked it from her coat pocket.

"Leave that office now!" Demetrio's mock-stern voice commanded.

She grinned. "You are *so* bossy. Is that how Italians treat their wives?"

"No. That is how Italians protect their loved ones who think of others before themselves."

"Protect," she sighed. "I like 'protect.'"

"Don't be late, *cara*." His voice had lowered, and she could hear the shouts of children and the rest of his family—and *hers* now—in the background.

She pushed the front door of the farmhouse open, and

was immediately swamped by the familiar warmth and smell of food, and shouts of laughter. "I wouldn't be late on Christmas Eve!" she called out to Demetrio who was frowning at his phone. He looked up, and his face was alight with happiness.

"Here she is!"

He walked over to her and swung her carefully around in his arms and kissed her.

"I told you she'd be home early." Ursula's father grinned at her as he accepted a refill of wine from Demetrio's father.

Demetrio brushed his lips against hers once more. "I have to watch out for her because she'd give all her time for free to the youth of Abbadia San Alexis if she could."

"Not now she's pregnant," her step-mother called out, red-faced from the Aga.

Ursula pulled away from Demetrio and went and kissed her step-mother who was stoically stirring the pot, just as Ursula had done the previous year. "How's it going, Dayna?"

Dayna sighed. "It's going, Ursula. Not sure where, though."

Ursula laughed. "You're doing better than I did."

Demetrio passed her a cup of tea, and she sat down beside Nonna, whom she kissed.

"A toast, Ursula," Nonna said. "Happy Christmas, everyone—especially to my newest daughter, who came to us by accident, at Christmas."

"To Ursula, and an accidental Christmas!"

THE END

That's the end of my Italian Romance series. If you'd like to read another of my romances, why not check out my Desert Kings series? It features sheikhs who are used to their every command being obeyed. Problem is, they fall in love with strong women with minds of their own!

Buy the first book in the Desert Kings series now!

Crown Prince Malek of Sumaira needs the respectability of a wife—fast. Or at least his country does. And his new assistant is happy to help him find one. After looking after her sick mother for years, the last thing Sophie wants is to be tied down. But will her good intentions survive working day in, day out, with the gorgeous Malek?

Wanted: A Wife for the Sheikh

Dear Reader,

Thank you for reading *An Accidental Christmas.* I hope you enjoyed it! Reviews are always welcome—they help me and they help prospective readers decide if they'd enjoy the book.

My other series include **Desert Kings, Sheikhs of Havilah, Secrets of the Sheikhs and Diamond Sheikhs** which feature sheikhs who are used to their every command being obeyed, strong women, a mystery or two, and exotic settings. And then there's my **British Billionaires** series which features three hard-hearted billionaires and three women who bring them to their knees! Read on for an excerpt to the first in the **Desert Kings** series—*Wanted: A Wife for the Sheikh.*

You can check out all my books on the following pages. And, if you'd like an email letting you know when my latest release has been published, you can sign up to my email list via my website—dianafraser.com.

Happy reading!

Diana

WANTED: A WIFE FOR THE SHEIKH

BOOK 1 OF DESERT KINGS

Crown Prince Malek of Sumaira needs a wife. Fast. Or at least his country does.

Malek was happy living the life of an international lawyer, but when his brother disappears he has no choice but to become ruler of one of the Middle East's most wealthy and turbulent countries. He needs respect, he needs stability, he needs a wife— preferably with no history—fast.

And Sophie, his new PA, is more than happy to help him find one. She's landed the dream job—well paid, lots of travel and no time for love. Computer-whizz Sophie has hardly left the house for the past few years while she's cared for her mother. And now, with her mother gone, she's determined never to be tied down again.

But will working day in, day out, with this Michael Fassbender clone make Sophie change her mind? Will the idea of being tied down by him become something she thinks about obsessively, something she needs to get out of her system before it's too late for either of them...

Excerpt

Malek lifted her hands to his lips and kissed them gently. He brushed his lips against her skin and looked into her eyes. She wanted her lips to replace her hands. She wanted him pressed against her, wanted his lips on hers, wanted to entwine her arms around him and never let go. Could she? Could she forget they had no future and live in the present and make her dreams a reality? Could she tell him how she felt? All it would take was one sign from him.

"Sophie," he breathed against her skin. "These past weeks have been made bearable only by you. And for that I thank you from the bottom of my heart."

Sophie's heart sank. He was grateful, that was all. She pulled her hand away from his and tried to ignore the fleeting look of hurt in his eyes. "You're welcome. You're paying me well for it." It pained her to see the shutter come over his face. But she had no choice. She felt things for him which weren't and could never be reciprocated. She had to survive, she had to protect herself.

"Of course." His ambiguous response could have meant many things. But from the look in his eye she saw he understood.

"Next week we must begin the process of selecting your new wife."

"My new wife," Malek said, with a bitterness which soured the atmosphere. He pulled away and walked across to the courtyard and stood looking over the city lights, hands thrust into his pockets. His white shirt gleamed in the dull light. "What the hell have I got myself into, eh, Sophie? A country I haven't lived in for a dozen years, a family I distanced myself from years ago, people who distrust me at best, and hate me at worst, and a marriage built on nothing but politics."

The shreds of self-protection Sophie had been trying to hold on to dissolved instantly as she witnessed his deep sense of helplessness and frustration. She went over to him and touched him on his shoulder. He twisted around instantly as if electrified. He gripped her hand and looked at her urgently.

"How can I do this, Sophie? How can I pretend to be this person I am not?"

She shook her head. "You can't pretend, Malek. But you can be the man you are. That man is more than ready to be king. And when you show that man to the world, they will love you and they will respect you, and you can be the king you want to be."

He drew her gently to him. His palms were warm against the small of her back. "Sophie," he murmured, just before he kissed her.

The kiss was nothing like Sophie had imagined during those long hot nights lying awake thinking of Malek. She could not have conceived how the intensity of his personality could have been so vividly expressed in the kiss; she could not have imagined how that intensity could have been tempered with a sensitivity that called to the very heart of her, unleashing her passion more effectively than any demands could have done.

The kiss grew more passionate as his tongue flicked over her lips, which she parted to allow him greater access. She groaned as he pulled her close against his hard body. The feel of his hand moving under her top against her heated skin only increased her need. With his other hand he thrust his fingers through her hair to tilt her head. She closed her eyes as his mouth moved from her head to her throat and lower.

A sudden flash of light made them both freeze.

"What the hell?" muttered Malek. There was another telltale flash of light. He muttered an expletive and tugged her top back over her exposed skin. He took her hand and pulled her away, into the privacy of their courtyard. "Damn, what the hell was I thinking?"

"Neither of us were thinking," Sophie said, as she adjusted her clothing. "Paparazzi?"

He sighed. "Without a doubt. What the hell have I done?" he repeated. "Flirtation is one thing, but that was an entirely different matter." He glanced at her. "I'm sorry, Sophie, I didn't mean to drag your name through the mud."

She gave an uncertain laugh. "Mud? It was a kiss. I think it would take more than a kiss to drag my name through the mud."

"You don't understand. They've been waiting for something like this. Waiting for me to lose control. And I very nearly did. I'm sorry." He looked around, agitated. "You should go."

She nodded. But didn't move. Was their intimacy to end like this?

"Goodnight," he said, as he stepped from her as if she could hurt him. She choked back a response and practically ran into her room, not stopping until she was inside with the door closed. She pulled the white silk curtains together and sat on her bed, looking blindly at the curtains, as if she could see through them, as if she could see Malek, still standing in the courtyard looking at her with that expression in his eyes that made her melt inside. But he wouldn't be. That moment had passed, shot dead by the flash of the paparazzi's camera.

She tried to regulate her breathing but, with the doors, windows, and curtains closed tight, she felt she couldn't breathe, despite the air conditioning. She felt claustrophobic without the sense that Malek was with her, aware of her, wanting her.

But it wasn't to be. He'd made that clear. Whatever he wanted, whatever he felt, they had no future together. Sophie crawled onto her bed without undressing and closed her eyes and held close the memory of his kiss, knowing it would be all she had of Malek to hold on to after she left Sumaira.

Buy Now!

ALSO BY DIANA FRASER

—British Billionaires—

The Billionaire's Contract Marriage
The Billionaire's Impossible CEO
The Billionaire's Secret Baby
British Billionaire Boxed Set (complete series)

—Diamond Sheikhs—

At the Sheikh's Command
At the Sheikh's Bidding
At the Sheikh's Pleasure
Diamond Sheikhs Boxed Set (complete series)

—Secrets of the Sheikhs—

The Sheikh's Revenge by Seduction
The Sheikh's Secret Love Child
The Sheikh's Marriage Trap
Secrets of the Sheikhs Boxed Set (complete series)

—The Sheikhs of Havilah—

The Sheikh's Secret Baby
Bought by the Sheikh
The Sheikh's Forbidden Lover

Surrender to the Sheikh

Taken for the Sheikh's Harem

The Sheikhs of Havilah Boxed Set (complete series)

Wanted: A Wife for the Sheikh

The Sheikh's Bargain Bride

The Sheikh's Lost Lover

Awakened by the Sheikh

Claimed by the Sheikh

Wanted: A Baby by the Sheikh

Desert Kings Boxed Set (1-3)

Desert Kings Boxed Set (4-6)

Desert Kings Boxed Set (complete series)

The Italian's Perfect Lover

Seduced by the Italian

The Passionate Italian

An Accidental Christmas

Italian Romance Boxed Set (complete series)

A Place Called Home

Secrets at Parata Bay

Escape to Shelter Springs

What you See in the Stars

Second Chance at Whisper Creek

Summer at the Lakehouse Café

The Mackenzies Boxed Set (Books 1-3)

The Mackenzies Boxed Set (Books 4-6)

The Mackenzies Complete Boxed Set

—Lantern Bay—

Yours to Give

Yours to Treasure

Yours to Cherish

Yours to Keep

Yours Forever

Yours to Love

Lantern Bay Box Set (Books 1-3)

Lantern Bay Box Set (Books 4-6)

The Lantern Bay Complete Boxed Set

—Medieval Romance—

Claiming his Lady

Seducing his Lady

Awakening his Lady

Norfolk Knights Boxed Set (1-3)

Defending his Lady

Honoring his Lady

ABOUT THE AUTHOR

I write romances with stories which make you turn the pages, and characters who feel real—whether they be sheikhs, British billionaires, medieval knights or everyday people whose lives are usually far from everyday (at least in my books).

A little about me...I'm an avid people watcher, hopeless romantic and dreamer who spends far too much time gazing out the window, imagining scenes where people struggle with life and emotions but always end up happily. Because, yes, I'm also an eternal optimist!

I live in beautiful New Zealand, just north of Wellington in a small village by the sea. It's here, in a sunny window seat overlooking the hills and trees, that I write my books.

Wherever you are in the world, welcome to my little corner, creating worlds where people struggle with life and emotions but are always rewarded with love and happiness in the end. Because that's non negotiable!

I hope you enjoy my books.

Diana

www.ingramcontent.com/pod-product-compliance
Lightning Source LLC
Chambersburg PA
CBHW021355150726
47989CB00005B/2257